Inferno:

A Chronicle of a
Distant World

INFERNO:

A Chronicle of a Distant World

Mike Resnick

A TOM DOHERTY ASSOCIATES BOOK
NEW YORK

INFERNO: A CHRONICLE OF A DISTANT WORLD

A Tor Book
Published by Tom Doherty Associates, Inc.
175 Fifth Avenue
New York, N.Y. 10010

Tor® is a registered trademark of Tom Doherty Associates, Inc.

Resnick, Michael D.
    Inferno / Mike Resnick.
        p. cm.
    "A Tom Doherty Associates book."
    ISBN 0-312-85437-4
    1. Life on other planets—Fiction.   I. Title.
    PS3568.E698I54   1993
    813'.54—dc20   93-26917
                                                              CIP

First edition: December 1993

Printed in the United States of America

0 9 8 7 6 5 4 3 2 1

To Carol, as always,

And to Gary Davis and Jamie Harrison,
lawyers in white hats

Contents

Foreword

There is a parable that Ugandans, white and black alike, sometimes tell when they sit around a campfire at the end of the day.

It seems that there was a scorpion who wished to cross a river. He saw a crocodile floating a few feet away and asked to be carried across the river on its back.

"Oh, no," said the crocodile firmly. "I know what you are. As soon as we're halfway across the river you'll sting me and I'll die."

"Why would I do that?" scoffed the scorpion. "If I sting you and you die, I'll drown."

The crocodile considered the scorpion's answer for a moment and then agreed to ferry him across the river. When they were halfway across, the scorpion stung the crocodile.

Fatally poisoned, barely able to breathe, the crocodile croaked, "Why did you do that?"

The scorpion thought for a moment, and then, just before he drowned, he answered, ''Because it's Africa.''

I have exercised my author's prerogative and related this anecdote to you only because it is an amusing story. It obviously has nothing at all to do with this novel, which is about the mythical world of Faligor rather than the very real nation of Uganda.

M.R.

Prologue

Y*ou wonder how these things happen.*
*You walk down the blood-drenched streets, make
your way between the skeletons of burnt-out buildings, try
not to stare with ghoulish fascination at the broken bodies
littering the landscape, and you keep repeating to yourself:
This is not what civilized beings do to each other.*

*You say it again and again, but the reality gives lie to
it. This is precisely what civilized beings have done to each
other. In fact, it is what they have done to themselves.*

*An infant wheezes in the shadows. It no longer has the
strength to scream. It is half-buried beneath the twisted
corpse of its mother, and since you are a doctor, you walk over
and tend to it as best you can, but you know it will be dead
in another ten minutes, half an hour at most. You estimate
that it has been lying beneath its mother's body for two days,
possibly three, given the state of its dehydration, and you
should be shocked and repelled, but it is nothing compared
to the sights you have already seen on this world, this
beautiful green and blue planet that once held such promise.*

You treat the worst of the infant's wounds, and since you have nothing to feed it, you lift it in your arms and carry it along with you, trying to make its last moments of life minimally more comfortable. Eyes, alien but sentient, peer out at you from behind broken doors and shattered windows. The figure of a looter darts through the shadows, realizes that you have seen it, and vanishes as quickly as it appeared.

The other members of your team begin gathering, their faces pale and grim. You hear the hum of a laser rifle a few streets away, then a scream, and then all is silence again.

"God!" says your commanding officer, as he rejoins the group. "How did it get this far out of hand?"

You notice that the infant has died, and you gently place it on the ground, in the shade.

"This is not what sentient beings do to one another," you repeat numbly.

"The Diamond of the Outer Frontier," mutters another officer. "Isn't that what they used to call it?"

"Once," answers your commanding officer. "A very long time ago."

You look up and down the blistered streets of the shattered city and shake your head in puzzlement. They were an ancient and civilized race, the inhabitants of this world. They loved the land, cherished the family, revered life. It has been said that they had codified the laws of their society when Man was still living in caves and hunting his dinner with wooden clubs and stone axes. They had happily joined the community of worlds and willingly vowed to adhere to its principles.

So you ask yourself again: How did they get from there to here?

And because in your entire experience, you have never seen a charnel house such as this, and devoutly hope never to see one again, you make it your business to find the answer.

1

DIAMOND

One

Three hundred dead kings waited with eternal patience as the khaki-clad woman approached the enclosure. Six hundred sightless eyes watched as she came to a halt before their successor. A slight breeze caused some of their weapons to rattle, some of their robes to stir, as they stood, silent and unmoving, the harsh sentinels of the current ruler's ancestral court, mute possessors of the accumulated wisdom of their race.

The emperor, his golden fur rippling in the bright sunlight, sat on a tall wooden stool, observing the woman. He displayed no fear, no apprehension, merely curiosity. A withered advisor stood directly behind him, while on each side of him, clad in brilliantly-hued ceremonial armour and feathered headdresses, were some fifty warriors, their axes at the ready, motionless as statues. They had formed an aisle for her approach, and now they closed ranks and formed a circle to contain her.

The woman bowed from the waist. The warriors tensed at the sudden motion, but the emperor merely inclined his head slightly.

"I have observed your progress for many hours," he said at last. "Who are you, and why have you come to the land of the Enkoti?"

"My name is Susan Beddoes," answered the woman, "and I come in peace. I carry no weapons."

"I know," he answered. "If you had brought weapons with you, you would not have lived to reach my kingdom." He paused. "Why did your ship land so far away?"

"I did not wish to frighten you."

"We have seen a ship before. It belonged to another, similar to you, but taller, who visited us many years ago."

Beddoes nodded. "His name was Wilson McConnell."

"He gave us many gifts."

"I have brought gifts as well. They are in my ship."

"How is it that you speak the language of the Enkoti?"

"I do not speak it," she replied, indicating a tiny device that pressed against her larynx. "What you hear is not my voice, but the voice of the mechanism that translates your words into my language and my words into yours. Though I hope, before long, to be able to converse without it."

"Ah," he said noncommittally.

"You do not seem impressed," said Beddoes.

The emperor shrugged, his golden fur rippling and

reflecting the sunlight. "Why should I be? It is just a toy."

"You've seen one before?"

"Yes."

The old advisor leaned forward and whispered something, and the emperor nodded almost imperceptibly.

"Let me tell you this, Susan Beddoes," continued the emperor. "I come from an unbroken line of three hundred sitates, and the most ancient of them had created codes of law and behavior for the Enkoti and imposed order upon our domain when the great river that flows to our west was little more than a stream. Neither I nor my people are children; we will not be treated as such."

"That was never my intention," answered Beddoes.

"I am the Sitate Disanko, the three hundred and first in my dynasty. I will be treated with the respect due my position."

"I meant no offense," said Beddoes. She gestured to the three hundred dead Enkoti, each perfectly preserved. "Are these your forebears?"

"That is correct." Disanko stared at her. "Wilson McConnell told me that you buried your dead in the ground. How can you pay respect to them when their bodies are eaten away by worms and insects?"

"That's a good question," admitted Beddoes.

"Then perhaps you will answer it."

"My race venerates the spirit, rather than the flesh that houses it."

"It is indeed the spirit that sets us above the animals," said Disanko, "but the spirit must have a home, or the Maker of All Things would not have provided each spirit with one."

"An interesting concept," said Beddoes. "I will think upon it."

"McConnell was an explorer, and a mapmaker," said Disanko, seeming to tire of the subject. "Are you also here to make maps?"

"No," she replied. "I am an exoentomologist."

"I do not understand the word."

"An entomologist studies insects," explained Beddoes. "An exoentomologist studies insects that live on worlds other than her own."

"You have come all this way to study insects?" said Disanko with an air of disbelief.

"Yes."

The sitate paused and stared at her through oblique, sky-blue eyes. "There are insects all over the planet. Why have you come to the heart of my kingdom?"

"I will need help with my field work," she replied. "McConnell's reports say that the Enkoti are the most powerful race on Faligor, so I have sought you out. I am willing to pay for your assistance."

"With what will you pay?"

"I have a line of credit at the Bank of Rockgarden," she replied. "I can pay in credits, New Stalin rubles, Maria Theresa dollars. . . ."

Disanko's thin lips pulled back from his teeth in what Beddoes hoped was a smile.

"Wilson McConnell explained money to me when he was here. It is a foolish concept."

"It is a concept that is in practice upon more than fifty thousand worlds," said Beddoes.

"That does not make it less foolish, only more widespread," answered Disanko. "Why should anyone work for something that has no value in itself?"

"It has value to *me*," she said.

The withered old advisor leaned forward and whispered to Disanko again. The sitate answered, the old advisor shook his head vigorously and said something more, and finally Disanko turned back to Beddoes.

"What have you to trade for our help?" asked the sitate.

Beddoes smiled, relieved. "I have medicines, and machines that will make your work easier. I have translating devices so that you can speak to members of other races. I have mutated seeds that will double your crop production. I have communication devices that will make it unnecessary for you to send a runner from one village to another with messages. I have gadgets that will tell you if there are rocks beneath a field before you break your plows on them." She paused. "I have things you've never dreamed of, Sitate Disanko."

"Do not be so certain that your trinkets are greater than a sitate's dreams," he cautioned her.

"If I have offended you, it is due to my ignorance of your customs, and I beg your forgiveness and understanding," said Beddoes.

"We will eat now," announced Disanko. "Then you will tell me exactly what your work entails, and how many of my people you will require, and for how long, and what you will trade for their services. Then I will consult with my ancestors, and we will eat and sleep again, and tomorrow morning I will give you my answer.''

"That will be acceptable," said Beddoes.

Disanko stared at her again. "I do not recall asking if it was acceptable. Your kingdom is many stars distant from here; you are in *my* kingdom now."

Beddoes bowed again. "I must return to my ship to get the goods I wish to trade. I can be back before dark."

"First you will eat with me," said Disanko firmly. "If it requires an extra day for me to make my decision, the insects will still be there."

Beddoes shrugged. "As you wish."

He shook his head. "As I *command*."

"When do we eat?" asked Beddoes.

"Soon," said Disanko. He stood up, and suddenly Beddoes became aware of the sounds of the village, the laughing and playing of children, the comings and goings of laborers, and she realized for the first time that her meeting with the sitate had taken place in total silence. "You may look around first, if you wish," said the sitate.

"Thank you. I'd very much like to."

Disanko summoned one of his warriors. "Her life is your life."

"I don't understand," said Beddoes.

"There are many wild animals beyond our city, and some of them are eaters of flesh. Tubito will protect you, to the point of sacrificing his life, if need be."

"That won't be necessary," said Beddoes.

"Let us hope that it is not necessary," said Disanko. "He has been a good and loyal servant, and I should be most displeased to lose him."

Beddoes studied the sitate, trying to determine whether he was issuing a threat or merely stating a fact, but his golden face disclosed no emotion, and finally she turned to Tubito, who looked questioningly at Disanko. The sitate nodded, and Tubito bowed and began leading her past Disanko's exquisitely preserved ancestors.

Eventually they reached a major avenue, and she followed him between rows of surprisingly complex wood and grass houses. Children came out to stare at her, and she noticed that, once away from Disanko, Tubito's entire demeanor had changed. He smiled, he spoke to the children, he waved to a number of the women who paused to watch them.

Suddenly she was conscious of the pungent odor of animals, and she saw that they were approaching a number of large, meticulously-constructed pens that housed the community's meat animals. Laced around the wooden bars were row upon row of thorns, obviously placed there to keep the domestic animals in and the predators out.

"Would you like to walk out beyond the city?" asked Tubito.

"If we have time," answered Beddoes.

"The sitate would not have sent me to accompany you if we did not," replied the Enkoti. He stared at her. "You are a female, are you not?"

"Yes."

"You must come from a very strange land," said Tubito. "Here no female other than his wives may address the sitate, and then never in public—and yet you spoke to him without fear."

"Among my race, males and females are considered equal," answered Beddoes.

"Then the males are the same size as the females?" asked Tubito.

"No, they are larger."

Tubito seemed about to say something, then changed his mind and began leading her around the corrals.

"You wish to ask something?" said Beddoes.

"I am trying to understand," he replied. "But I do not wish to cause offense."

"Ask your question. It won't offend me."

He stopped walking and turned to her. "If males are larger and stronger than females, you cannot defeat them in combat. Therefore, I wonder why they consider you to be their equals." He paused, frowning. "Unless you are stronger, even though they are larger."

"We are not stronger."

"Then . . . ?" He shrugged in puzzlement.

"We are their mental and spiritual equals," said Beddoes. "And since we have machines to do our work for us, and even fight our wars for us, physical strength is not a measure of worth."

He considered her statement for a long moment. "That is most interesting," he said at last, trying to comprehend a world in which the mental was more highly valued than the physical.

"Surely you have the equivalent among the En-koti," continued Beddoes. "For example, the old one who whispered to Disanko is weak and frail, but I notice that the sitate values his advice."

"True," admitted Tubito. "But he is the Oracle."

"Can no female become an oracle?"

"No female *has* been one," said Tubito. "But I suppose it is possible. There is old Marapha, who never leaves her house, but forecasts the rains."

"You see?" said Beddoes with a smile. "Perhaps we are not so different after all."

"Perhaps," said Tubito. "I wonder if I might ask you more about your city?"

"If I, in turn, can ask you more about yours," she replied. "For example, how many Enkoti cities are there, and how far does your kingdom extend?"

"If you will climb the highest peak of the Hills of Heaven," answered Tubito, pointing to a mountain range far to the west, "everything that you can see, from there to the Bortai River, belongs to the En-koti."

They passed a grove of fruit trees. Tubito pulled down a reddish citrus fruit, peeled it with a knife, and handed it to her.

"I don't know if it is safe for me to eat it," said Beddoes.

"McConnell ate them with no ill effects," answered Tubito. "In fact, when he left, he took many of them with him."

She held it up to her face, sniffed at it cautiously, and then took a small bite.

"It's very sweet."

"It gives you strength," said Tubito. He stared at her expectantly.

"I like it."

Tubito seemed relieved, and pulled down two more. One he handed to her, and another he bit into, without removing the outer peel.

"What do your people eat?" he asked.

"A little of everything: meat, fish, birds, vegetables, fruit," she answered.

"And milk?"

"When we are very young."

"*We* drink milk every day," he said. "It makes us strong."

"I'm sure it does."

"Then why do you drink it only when you are young?"

She tried to explain the concept of vitamins and balanced diets to him, but while he listened politely, she could tell that he understood almost nothing of what she said.

Before long they found themselves in waist-high grass, and Tubito moved in front of her and began walking very slowly, his keen eyes scanning the area.

"What's the matter?" asked Beddoes.

"This is the domain of the Plainstalker, which can kill an animal four times its own size. It is much the same color as the grass, and strikes swiftly and silently. Probably there are none nearby, for otherwise our penned animals would have scented them and become uneasy, but one cannot take chances with

Plainstalkers.'' He paused and turned to her. ''Perhaps you would rather return to the city?''

To continue virtually unarmed in these surroundings would have verged on the suicidal, and while Beddoes carried a molecular imploder that could turn any carnivore to jelly in a fraction of a second, she had no desire to show off the state of her weaponry, so she nodded her acquiescence.

''Perhaps if you stay long enough, you can watch our young warriors embark on a Plainstalker hunt,'' suggested Tubito.

''Do you hunt them to protect your stock animals?'' she asked.

Tubito shook his head. ''No male may take a wife without killing a Plainstalker in physical combat.''

''I think I might enjoy watching such a hunt,'' she said. ''Speaking of animals, on my walk from my ship to your city, I passed some huge herbivores, standing twice as tall as an Enkoti at the shoulder. I'm surprised they haven't eaten the vegetation down.''

''Often they do,'' answered Tubito. ''But then it rains, and everything grows again.''

''How often does it rain?''

''Almost every afternoon.''

They made their way back to the village through a profusion of flowers, shrubbery and fruit trees. Beddoes stopped twice to admire the colorful avians that flew overhead, and once to examine a small ten-legged purple-and-white insect that Tubito caught for her.

''Thank you,'' she said as he handed it to her.

"The sitate says you are interested in insects. I am happy to help."

"That was very thoughtful of you."

"I do the sitate's bidding," he answered. "Though I am glad that it makes you happy."

"Tell me about him."

"The sitate?"

"Yes," said Beddoes.

"He has been a good ruler," replied Tubito. "He is firm but compassionate, and the justice he metes out is swift and fair. Under Disanko our kingdom has prospered, and he has actually fought very few wars with our neighbors, preferring to negotiate."

"From a position of strength, of course."

"One cannot negotiate from a position of weakness," said Tubito.

They found Disanko waiting for them, and she was immediately ushered into his dwelling, a multi-chambered structure that seemed to go on forever. Just when she was wondering where the dining room was, they emerged into a courtyard that was surrounded by thorn fencing, with warriors standing guard every ten feet, and she realized that the tour of the "palace" had been performed simply to impress her.

She was led to one side of a low, hand-carved wooden table, while Disanko stood opposite her.

"Wilson McConnell ate our meat animals when he was here, and suffered no ill effects," announced the sitate. "Therefore, I assume they will not harm you." He clapped his hands, and two females staggered in bearing a huge tray containing more meat than Beddoes could have eaten in a month. "Please sit down."

Beddoes seated herself on a small stool, much lower than Disanko's, as the females bowed and left.

"You seem uncomfortable," he noted.

"I am," she admitted.

"You may sit on the floor, if you prefer." He paused. "I know you would prefer a higher stool, but there is only one sitate's chair, and no one else may sit upon it."

She considered her options and lowered herself to the floor. Before either she or Disanko could take a bite of anything, one of the warriors stepped forward, pulled out his dagger, and cut off a piece of meat. He chewed it thoroughly, swallowed it, and stepped back to his position against the thorn wall. Then another warrior approached and ate a small purple fruit. This went on until every variety of food had been tasted by one of the warriors.

"A precaution," explained Disanko. "I am not without my enemies, those who wish to become sitate and those who simply wish for any sitate other than myself. I may someday be killed in battle, but at least I know I will not be poisoned."

A colorful avian, about the size of a large crow, flew down from an overhanging branch and perched on the corner of the table. Disanko flipped a piece of fruit onto the ground, and the avian swooped down, grabbed the morsel in its claws, and, screeching happily, flew back to its perch in the tree.

If Beddoes expected to speak to Disanko about her mission or anything else, she was disappointed, for

the sitate began eating and never said a word or
looked up until he was finished. When he had finished, the tray was taken away, and a lovely young
female, just approaching maturity, entered the area
and began grooming Disanko's furry face with her
fingers. She left a moment later, Disanko stood up,
and Beddoes got to her feet.

"You may spend the night in your ship," he announced.

"I thought you wanted me here," she said.

"I did, but the affairs of state intervene. My ambassador has returned from the land of the Traja, and
I must confer with him. You will return in the morning, and then we will negotiate for my people's services. Tubito will accompany you."

"I will be happy to have Tubito's company, but if
you require him for any other duties, I am quite
capable of making my way to my ship on my own."

"When you are in the country of the Enkoti, you
are under my protection," said Disanko. "Tubito
will accompany you."

The sitate's manner said that the meal and inter-
view were both over, and Beddoes merely bowed and
waited for him to leave. Then she stepped outside,
where she found Tubito waiting for her.

The trek to her ship took a little more than two
hours. They passed numerous herds of herbivores,
some huge and ponderous, some small and swift,
and once he grabbed her by the shoulder and pointed
to a tree limb about a quarter of a mile distant. She
saw a flicker of motion, a flash of crimson skin and
brilliant white teeth, and then nothing, as the crea-

ture vanished behind some foliage that she would have sworn couldn't have hidden half of it from view.

They crossed the same three streams she had crossed in the morning, each lined with bushes laden with scarlet-and-gold berries, passed a grove of flowering trees, and finally arrived at the ship.

"Will you be going home now?" asked Beddoes.

He shook his head. "I will sleep outside your ship."

"What will you eat?"

He reached into a pouch that was suspended from his waist and pulled out a piece of dried meat, holding it up for her to see.

"If it rains, just open the hatch and make yourself at home."

"That is very kind of you," he replied, "but I am used to rain."

"There's no need to be uncomfortable."

"I appreciate your offer, Susan Beddoes, but I serve the sitate, and the sitate has ordered me to protect you. If danger threatens, it will not come from within your ship."

She entered her ship, going straight to the cargo area to select the gifts and trade items she would bring with her tomorrow. After sorting through them and packing them neatly, she went into the galley, ordered it to prepare dinner for her, and sat down to record her day's activities in her log.

A few hours later, as she prepared to go to sleep in her cabin, the computer informed her that a message was coming in over the subspace radio. She had it transferred to the cabin and sat up.

"Attention, *Crystal Wing*, do you read?" said a masculine voice, crackling with static. "Attention, *Crystal Wing*, do you read?"

"This is the *Crystal Wing*, Susan Beddoes commanding, nine days out of Amazonia, currently at rest on Brazzi II, local name Faligor."

"Good evening, Susan." There was a brief pause. "At least, according to my charts, I *think* it's evening where you are."

"It is, Arthur."

"Well?" asked Arthur Cartright, Assistant Secretary of the Republic's Department of Cartography, which was located on the distant world of Caliban. "What's your first impression?"

"McConnell was right: it's a beautiful world. Temperate, fertile, unpolluted. You get the feeling that you could toss a packet of seeds—any kind of seeds—out the hatch, and by tomorrow morning there'd be a garden in full bloom."

"And the natives?"

"I'd say they're a bit more sophisticated than your run-of-the-mill aboriginals—they're working with metals, and they seem to possess a complex social structure—but technologically they're quite primitive."

"Friendly?"

"They seem to be."

"Better and better," said Cartright. "Any military capability?"

"None that I could see," replied Beddoes. "Of

course, we're going under that assumption that the Enkoti are the most advanced of the various tribes, and McConnell could be wrong about that—but they do rule a vast amount of land, and no one seems to be threatening to take it away from them. In fact, the ruler made some reference to meeting his ambassador to some other kingdom."

"Ambassador, eh? They *are* a little more advanced than McConnell's reports would indicate." Cartright cleared his throat. "So much the better. It looks like we chose the right world."

"That's my initial impression," agreed Beddoes. "Of course, we'll need a few more months to be sure."

"We don't have that luxury," replied Cartright. "We're operating on a very tight schedule. I don't know how much longer Breshinsky can hold on to her job at the Department of Alien Affairs, and if Nkomo succeeds her, as seems likely, we're not going to have much time before he decides to call in the Navy. We've opened six mining worlds near Faligor; the Republic desperately needs an agricultural world to supply them. Also, while McConnell's analysis wasn't as thorough as we might have wished, it looks like Faligor has more than its share of gold, silver and fissionable materials, especially in that mountain range to the west of you."

"I thought they were going to let us open this world *our* way," said Beddoes.

"Half the politicians on Deluros don't understand what our function really is," said Cartright, frustration creeping into his voice. "To them, the Department of Cartography is just some huge, overfunded mapmaking institute. They still don't realize that we're the ones who determine how and where Man is to expand in the galaxy, who tell the Navy where to set up its lines of supply and defense. They're already resentful that we determine which planets the Republic assimilates, and now that we're also trying to show them *how,* they're up in arms."

"You'd think after all the messes that Alien Affairs has had to clean up, they'd be thrilled to have someone besides the military open up some worlds."

"I wish it was that simple, but we're invading their turf, so to speak, and when you deal with power brokers of this magnitude there are always problems," said Cartright.

"So what happens next?"

"We speed up our schedule."

"But we'd planned each step so carefully," protested Beddoes.

"Susan, we no longer have the luxury of being as careful as we'd like. I'd hoped to spend ten years carefully assimilating Faligor into the Republic, but I'd say we have three at the outside."

"So it's gone from being our best hope to our last one, right?" said Beddoes bitterly.

"Let's not be negative, Susan. We've learned from our mistakes on Peponi and Lodin XI and Rockgarden. If we didn't think we could do a better job of it, we wouldn't have lobbied for permission." He sighed deeply. "There are two million oxygen worlds yet to be opened up in the galaxy. Our computers tell us that from ten to twelve thousand of them will possess sentient life. If we can make Faligor a model of how to assimilate such worlds, maybe we can save some of them—and ourselves— the problems we've caused elsewhere.''

''All right,'' said Beddoes. ''What do we do next?''

''I''m dispatching a contact team of two hundred Men to Faligor the day after tomorrow. It will contain the usual—doctors, agricultural experts, geologists, aquaculturalists, everything except military advisors. They'll arrive about ten days from now.''

''And what do you want me to do in the meantime?'' asked Beddoes.

''Nothing special,'' replied Cartright. ''Learn what you can about their society. Prepare them for our arrival, and see if you can get them to look forward to it with some enthusiasm. Tell them about the wonderful inventions and medicines we're bringing them. In short,'' he concluded wryly, ''just be an exemplary representative of your race. Hell, you can even continue to go around collecting bugs if you want; after all, that's your specialty.''

''What do I tell them about the farmland?''

''I don't quite follow you.''

''You need a farming planet,'' Beddoes pointed out. ''How much of their land are you going to appropriate?''

''We're not going to *appropriate* anything. If we have to, we'll find some land no one is living on or working—but I'd much rather try to introduce a monied economy to Faligor and let the inhabitants

sell their produce to the mining worlds." He paused
again, then said passionately, "Just this once, we're
going to do it right. Man has enough subjects; he
needs some partners."

"Will you be coming yourself?" asked Beddoes.

"As soon as I can," answered Cartright. "We're
currently engaged in military actions in six different
sectors, and the Department of Energy is in urgent
need of another dozen mining worlds, and we're
only halfway done charting the Albion Cluster. If
I'm lucky, I might make it there in about three Stan-
dard months. Probably four—and that's if nothing
else crops up."

"Do you want me to make daily reports until your
team arrives?"

"No, I only want you to do it when it's convenient.
The last thing we want them to think is that you're
sneaking off to the ship each night to plot an invasion. Anything you don't tell me you can tell the
team leader."

"All right," said Beddoes. "Is there anything
else?"

"No, just do a good job," said Cartright. "There
aren't that many Edens in the galaxy, and we've
destroyed quite enough of them. It's time we left one
intact."

He broke the connection.

Two

The contact team landed on schedule. Within a week a vaccination clinic had been set up for the Enkoti, and in a months's time there were more than two dozen other clinics in operation among the Rizzali, the Traja, the Bolimbo, and all the other tribes.

The land proved as fertile as Susan Beddoes had hoped, and the team appropriated some thirty thousand square miles of untilled soil for human farmers. When some of the sitates objected, emissaries were dispatched to make restitution; the Traja and Bolimbo accepted tractors and mutated seeds, but Disanko, who had been studying Men as closely as they had been studying him, insisted upon currency.

Within three months there were tarmac roads connecting the capitals of the major tribes, and some two hundred human teachers were imported to teach both the children and the adults the rudiments of science, mathematics and the Terran language, which was the official language of the Republic and was fast becoming the *lingua franca* of the galaxy.

Then, six months after Beddoes had first landed, a discovery was made that brought Arthur Cartright to Faligor ahead of schedule. He landed at the temporary spaceport, got right into a small airplane, and took off. He returned that evening and immediately summoned a dozen of his most trusted aides to the hastily-erected building that momentarily served as humanity's headquarters.

Beddoes was among the invitees, and she filed into a large meeting room along with the other staff members. Cartright was waiting for them, standing stiffly in front of the chairs that had been lined up to face him. He was a tall, lean man, exquisitely dressed, with soft brown eyes and shaggy, unkempt gray-brown eyebrows, an aquiline nose, and a narrow mouth. He seemed uneasy, as if he were more used to doing his business on the vidphone or via subspace radio, as indeed he was. When all of his aides had taken their seats, he cleared his throat and began to speak.

"Before I get to the purpose of this meeting, I want to take this opportunity to tell you that I think you've done an excellent job thus far. We've made far more progress than even I had hoped for."

"The jasons get all the credit for that, sir," said the woman in charge of coordinating the medical efforts. "You couldn't ask for a friendlier, more intelligent, more pliable race to work with."

"Jasons?" repeated Cartright.

She smiled. "That's our name for them. Because of their golden fleece."

"Very good," said Cartright, returning her smile. "I approve. Unless they object, that is."

"They don't seem to mind it at all."

"Fine." He paused awkwardly. "Anyway, as I said, I think you've all done a remarkable job thus far." He fumbled with his pocket for a moment, then withdrew a hand computer and studied it briefly. "And now for the reason I've called this meeting. As you are aware, we chose Faligor because we knew it to be a rich agricultural world, with an ample water supply, an ideal climate, and a populace that we felt we could work with." He looked at the computer again, then put it back in his pocket. "Well, it turns out that Faligor is even richer than we had anticipated. I have just come back from the mountain range known as the Hills of Heaven, and it appears that they are honeycombed with exceptionally rich veins of gold and silver, as well as a not-inconsiderable supply of fissionable materials. Furthermore, in the desert south and west of the mountains we have already discovered three diamond pipes, with the possibility of still more to be found."

There was a brief buzz of excitement, and Cartright waited for it to subside.

"This means that Faligor can more than pay its own expenses, right from the start," he continued. "Not only will it be able to export food to the nearby mining worlds, but it may itself become one of the richest mining worlds in this sector. This presents us with enormous opportunities—but it also poses a problem that I wish to discuss with you, and hopefully to resolve before I leave in two days."

"We can't let the Republic in," said Constantine Talat, the burly medic in charge of the Enkoti vaccination program. "You let their miners set foot on Faligor, and within a month we'll have the Navy running the place. They'll conscript the jasons to work in the mines, and it'll be Rockgarden all over again."

"It was never my intention to invite the Republic to Faligor," answered Cartright, his nervousness gone now that he was addressing himself to his speciality. "We have made Faligor a Protectorate, not a colony. The Navy will only come in if our people are endangered." He paused. "There is one exception to that. If word gets out about what we've discovered and we are not exploiting the planet's riches to the Republic's satisfaction, then absolutely nothing Cartography can do will prevent them from moving in."

"So what you're saying is that we've got to start working the mines immediately," said Talat.

"I'm saying that *some*one has got to," answered Cartright. "I'm very loath to import human miners, because the Navy will insist on protecting them . . . and they won't *need* protection unless the Navy shows up and begins flexing its muscles, as it is inclined to do. So my question is this: are the jasons sophisticated enough to work with our mining equipment?"

"Not a chance," answered an educator. "They have no written language, and were even ignorant of the orbit of their planet until we arrived. They're bright, and most of them are eager learners, but it'll be years before they can deal with the computers and sophisticated machinery required for a full-scale mining operation."

"More to the point," added Victoria Domire, the head of the economic team, "none of them except the Enkoti has even the most rudimentary understanding of money. If you plan to work them in the mines, there's no way you can pay them. That means you'll have to conscript them, which is just the kind of situation we want to avoid."

"All right," said Cartright. "Those are pretty much the answers I had anticipated." He looked around the room. "Now, has anyone got any suggestions?"

Beddoes waited until she saw that no one else had any intention of speaking, and then raised her hand.

"The moles," she said.

"I beg your pardon?" said Cartright.

"Moles," she repeated. "I don't know their official name. They're the inhabitants of Socrates IV. Humanoid, oxygen-breathing, assimilated into the Republic for more than two centuries. They're highly skilled laborers who hire out to any world that can pay them. I ran into a group of them on Alpha Santori II."

"Do they work mines?" asked Victoria Domire.

"That's their specialty," answered Beddoes. "That's why we call them moles: because they spend so much of their time underground."

"We'd need a *lot* of them," said Domire.

"It's a big planet," said Beddoes.

"I'll take your suggestion under consideration,"
said Cartright. "In fact, if no one comes up with a
better one by morning, I'll almost certainly act on
it." He paused. "Now, are there any other questions
or problems anyone wishes to discuss with me?"

So many hands arose that Cartright was taken
aback. "I think the best way to handle this is for me
to meet with each department head in my office. In
the meantime, keep up the good work." He turned to
Beddoes. "Please come with me, Susan. I'd like to
speak to you first."

She followed him out of the meeting room, down
a long corridor that led to the office he had comman-
deered for himself when he first arrived. It contained
a desk, a small but powerful computer, and two
chairs, as well as a holographic map of Faligor.

"You've spent as much time among the jasons as
anyone, Susan," said Cartright. "So tell me—how
much resentment will there be if we import, say, fifty
thousand moles to work the mines?"

"I don't know," answered Beddoes. "They don't
seem to resent *us*, but—"

"But what?"

"But they can see that we're here to help them. I
don't know if they'll understand what the moles are
here for."

"Do you think that will make a difference?"

"Not at first."

"Then when?" persisted Cartright.

"When they realize that we're shipping valuable
materials off their planet and they're not getting any
revenues from them."

"That was never my intention. As I said, we need partners, not subjects."

Beddoes sighed deeply. "I don't know that that will make a difference."

"Please elaborate."

"Four months ago these people were living in the Stone Age . . . or, at best, the Bronze Age. Suddenly we're educating them and vaccinating them and showing them how to use farm machinery, and that's all well and good, but I think asking them to understand abstracts like a galactic economy and our need for fissionable materials is asking too much too soon. They can understand steel—after all, it makes better spears—but how can they understand the need for diamonds, especially industrial ones? The sitates will take our money, since they have no way of knowing which metals are worth money or how to sell them, but eventually they're going to feel that we are somehow betraying them by shipping these materials to *our* people, rather than showing *their* people how to use them and why they're worth so much to us."

"A point well-taken," said Cartright. "I can see that we cannot simply turn the mines over to the moles, or any other race. We'll have to get the jasons to give us some of their people to learn the procedures. Perhaps within a few years we can even have some of them acting in supervisory positions." He paused thoughtfully. "And it might be a good idea to ship the brightest of them to some of the Republic worlds for their education. Not that we won't have fine educational facilities here, but I want them to be able to come back and tell their people about what's out there, who we are, how we function."

Beddoes considered his statement for a moment, then shrugged. "I suppose it could work out," she said without enthusiasm.

"You sound dubious."

"The jasons are a wonderful species," she said. "They're bright, they're industrious, they're intelligent. Eventually I think they can be everything you hope they'll be."

"But?" said Cartright. "There's always a 'but'."

"But I think you're rushing them."

"We have no choice but to rush them. This world has to serve as a model for assimilation."

"I don't see that moving an entire race out of the bush and into the Galactic Era in one generation makes an ideal model." She paused. "My closest friend among the Enkoti, a warrior named Tubito, attained what I shall call his manhood by killing a huge carnivore with a spear not three years ago. He has many admirable qualities, not the least of which are his curiosity and intelligence, but you can't put him into a tunic and sit him down in front of a computer—not this year, not in ten years, possibly not ever. He could be the Copernicus or Galileo of his race, but he squats outside in the rain and eats strips of dried meat that he rips off with his bare hands."

"But his children can be assimilated as easily as yours or mine could," said Cartright.

"Probably," said Beddoes. "If they grew up in a human household."

"Your doubts are logged and noted," said Cartright. "But we simply haven't got the time. You've seen what's happened to other worlds when the Republic, with the best of intentions, tried to colonize them. Faligor is our last best chance to prove to them that there's a better way, to show them that the carrot works better than the stick. We're asking a lot of the jasons, I know, but they seem a bright and willing race, and the rewards will be commensurate with their effort. And, of course, the alternative is considerably worse."

"Well," said Beddoes. "You asked for my opinion. I gave it to you."

"And I thank you for it, Susan—and especially for your suggestion about the moles. Now, since I'm here for a limited time, I think I'd better speak with my other experts."

Realizing she had been dismissed, Beddoes got to her feet. She walked to the door, then stopped and turned to Cartright.

"May I make one final suggestion?"

"Certainly."

"I've only counted two alien psychologists among your experts," she said. "If you're going to accelerate the jasons' march to civilization, I'd import a hell of a lot more of them if I were you."

Three

Despite all of Susan Beddoes' doubts, Faligor worked.

There was no show of resentment at the importation of some three hundred thousand moles on long-term mining contracts.

Jason and Man worked side-by-side in the fields, taming the land and exporting more than enough food in the first six months so that the nearby mining worlds were no longer dependent upon any other source.

The seas proved to be as rich in protein as the soil was in minerals, and before long the fishing and aquaculture industries were also able not just to feed the populace but also to export their products as well.

No less a personage than Johnny Ramsey, the former Secretary of the Republic, came for a hunting safari, spent some time preaching his brand of democracy to the jasons, and solemnly declared that Faligor was the Diamond of the Outer Frontier.

Seventeen Republic worlds planned to open embassies on Faligor, each of them intent upon setting up trade relations with either the miners or the farmers or both.

At Disanko's invitation, Men built the city of Romulus on Enkoti soil, and made it their headquarters. Within a year the neighboring city of Remus was built on the shores of a large inland lake.

When Disanko died suddenly, stricken by a virus, he was succeeded by his son, Tantram, who immediately vowed to work closely with the Republic to bring its benefits to all of his people. His first act was to use the money Disanko had stockpiled to create Tantrum University on the outskirts of Romulus, and he established a trust fund that was sufficient to hire the finest human academics to staff it.

Cartright was elated at the way things were progressing, so much so that he purchased a large tract of land from the Rizzali and built a house on it with the intention of retiring to Faligor when his contract with the Department of Cartography expired.

Beddoes herself remained on the planet. When Cartography suggested it was time to move on, she resigned and signed up with one of the local safari companies, which had sprouted like weeds after Ramsey's visit and his subsequent book extolling the virtues of Faligor. She had no interest in or talent for hunting, but she acted as a guide for holo safaris, and spent her spare time pursuing her avocation. During her first two years on Faligor she had identified, catalogued, and named more than three thousand species of insects.

She was pleased to see that her passion for entomology, if it didn't exactly infect her fellow Men, at least caused most of them to bring her any insect they hadn't seen before, rather than grind it into the dirt. Once she began naming them after their discoverers, she found to her amusement that her fellow safari guides would bring insects to her by the dozens, and would make sure she knew how to spell their names before they left.

Since she still had friends in the Cartography Department, and since Faligor was still in the process of being mapped, she frequently went out with them on their surveys, just for the pleasure of seeing new areas of her adopted world. There were vast flatlands filled with herbivores, which had picked up such Terran nicknames as Thunderbulls, Tanbucks, Candystripes, and Skyjumpers. There were impenetrable rain forests, a huge central desert, and a number of mountain ranges, the most impressive of which was the snow-capped Hills of Heaven, the slopes of which were home to huge numbers of primates and avians.

There were some twenty-seven distinct tribes on the planet, all of them living on the one major continent. Each had several subgroups, and it was virtually impossible for any Man or jason to learn more than a handful of the hundred-plus languages, but at various times almost every tribe had been conquered by the now-decimated Maringo tribe, which had fallen upon hard times and numbered less than two thousand members, and most of the tribes spoke some variation of Maringo in addition to their native dialect. The Sitate Tantram decreed that all of his citizens must also learn Terran, and not to be out-done, the sitates of the other tribes followed suit, so that before long there were two planetary languages. Terran became the language of state, used for formal occasions and when dealing with offworlders, while Maringo was preferred when the jasons spoke infor-mally among themselves.

Within three years there were boreholes in every village, allowing the jasons access to water in times of drought, and modern farming methods had been adopted by all of the jason tribes. Before long huge hotels towered above Romulus and Remus, and hunting concessions were replaced by game parks in order to attract even greater numbers of tourists.

Faligor had come so far so quickly, had adapted itself to Man's vision so completely, that Beddoes found herself half-expecting the planet to be visited by some disaster, if only to chastise Man for his ambition. No world could be this perfect, this tran-quil and peaceful, this close to paradise. Oh, to be sure, the Rizzali and Traja had a minor border dis-pute that erupted into warfare, but when the Repub-lic's representatives moved in to mediate, only eleven jasons had been killed. And a particularly virulent form of skin disease, not totally unlike smallpox, had surfaced among the tribes living on the eastern savannah, but it took the human doctors less than a month to isolate the virus and only an-other three weeks to come up with a vaccine. Johnny

Ramsey came back for two more hunting safaris, accompanied, as always, by two or three dozen members of the press, and word of Faligor spread throughout the galaxy.

It was on Ramsey's final safari that the Sitate Tantram went out hunting with him, and was badly gored by a huge amphibian known as a Riverkiller. The medics managed to save his life, but he became an invalid, and turned over the kingship of his people to his younger brother, a Terranphile who took the name of the Sitate Robert August Tantram II.

The new sitate spoke exquisite Terran, had been schooled on the university planet of Aristotle, and had a passion for Terran history, fast vehicles, and human clothing. He built a huge theater in the center of Romulus and imported the finest human stage, opera and ballet companies. He also funded a museum dedicated to works of human art, and a publishing house committed to translating the oral traditions of the Enkoti into Terran.

He took too many human stimulants, and drove too many fast human vehicles, and looked just a little bit silly wearing formal human clothing, but Emperor Bobby, as the human populace dubbed him, was both popular with his people and a willing co-developer of his world with its human contingent.

He broke with many Enkoti traditions: he no longer held court in the presence of his ancestors, but now presided over the business of his people in an impressive white building he had built for that purpose. He renounced the religion of his people and converted, in quick order, to Christianity and Islam, and was currently a practitioner of the Hindu faith. Though nicotine had no effect whatsoever upon his metabolism, he became a heavy smoker, importing his cigars and cigarettes from distant Antarres.

He staged elaborate entertainments for his retainers and his human friends. One month he would sponsor an imported symphony orchestra, another month there would be a tripodal alien magician from Hesporite III. Once he flew his entire party out to watch the capture of a small herd of Thunderbulls for the zoo world of Serengeti.

The evening that he dropped his bombshell was at another of his many entertainments, this the first boxing match between a jason and a human. He had imported Billy Wycynski, the heavyweight champion of Sirius V, to fight Gama Labu, the huge Rizzali warrior who had thus far beaten all comers.

Susan Beddoes wasn't especially interested in boxing, but one didn't refuse an invitation from Emperor Bobby, so she dressed in what she hoped was an appropriate semiformal outfit and showed up at the designated time.

About two hundred Men and jasons were there, including Arthur Cartright, who was on a business trip to Faligor, and Beddoes noted with approval that some fifteen or twenty red-skinned moles were also in attendance. Bobby had torn down his brother's former domicile, and erected an impressive human-style palace in its place. His three hundred and one ancestors were discreetly hidden from view, as if he considered them an embarrassment. A boxing ring had been constructed in the middle of his newly-grown and meticulously-cropped lawn, surrounded by perhaps fifty tables, with more than one hundred uniformed jasons serving as waiters and ushers. Off to the left were extensive formal gardens, and just beyond them Beddoes could see some dwellings that had existed when she first arrived among the Enkoti: they were no more squalid or primitive now than then, but they seemed more so because of their proximity to the sitate's new residence.

"Susan!" said Emperor Bobby when he saw her. "I'm so glad you could come!"

Beddoes was taken aback by his greeting, as she hadn't exchanged twenty sentences with him since he ascended the throne, but he greeted her as if they were close personal friends and rattled on for a few minutes about insects, until his gaze fell upon some other newcomer and he went off to greet him.

She heard a low chuckle behind her, and turned to find herself facing Cartright.

"If he wasn't already the emperor, I'd swear our Bobby was running for office," he said.

"He does tend to overdo it," agreed Susan.

"That's the politician in him," said Cartright, an amused smile on his face. "He's quite something, isn't he?"

"Quite."

Cartright looked over the tables. "There don't seem to be any place cards or seating designations," he noted. "I suspect Bobby must have attended a garden party when he was offworld, and totally forgot how he knew where to sit. Shall we appropriate a table for ourselves?"

Beddoes nodded, and Cartwright led her to an empty table.

"I have no idea why I'm here," she said as she sat down. "I don't know anything about boxing," she said.

"You're here because Bobby likes to impress his human visitors," answered Cartright. "As for boxing, it's really very simple. Two Men—or in this case, a Man and a jason—get into the ring and try to kill each other."

"I wish he'd invited me to the symphony instead."

"*I* wish he'd imported someone with poorer credentials than this Wycynski fellow. It would do wonders for the jasons' self-esteem if their boxer could win."

"Maybe he can," said Beddoes without much interest.

"I hear he's good, but he's never faced an opponent of this quality before," said Cartright. "I don't give him much of a chance." He looked off to his right. "Oh-oh. Prepare yourself. It looks like we're to be joined by the royal presence."

Emperor Bobby walked up and seated himself next to them. "I hope you don't mind if I join you?"

"Not at all, Your Majesty," said Cartright, rising to his feet until Bobby had seated himself. "After all, it's your party."

"A charming expression," said Bobby pleasantly. He paused. "I notice you're not drinking. May I suggest the cognac? It's an excellent label, imported from the Cygni system."

He signalled to a waiter, who approached, opened a bottle, and poured out three glasses.

"To your good health, Your Majesty," said Cartright, raising his glass.

"I have a better toast," said Bobby, lifting his own glass.

"I should like to hear it," replied Cartright.

"Very well, then," said Bobby. He rose to his feet and waited until he had everyone's attention. "My friends," he said in a loud voice, "I propose a toast: to the swift and happy marriage of Faligor and the Republic."

There was wild applause from the jasons, and more restrained clapping from the humans.

"I beg your pardon, Your Majesty," said Cartright when Bobby had seated himself once again, "but I don't think I fully understood your toast. Relations between the Republic and Faligor have never been better."

"True," said Bobby. "That is why I think it is time for us to be given full membership."

"You will be, in time," said Cartright. "But let's not rush things."

"Why not?" asked Bobby with a disarming smile.

"I realize it seems an excellent idea to you, Your Majesty," continued Cartright. "But I urge you to consider your position as a Protectorate: you pay no taxes, your people are not conscripted into the military, you receive massive aid, the Republic supports your produce prices . . ."

"You make it sound like being a Protectorate is

better than being an equal partner," said Bobby. "Why do I have trouble believing that?"

"Believe me, Your Majesty, when Faligor is ready to join the Republic, you will be invited and accepted. But your literacy rate is less than fifteen percent, Tantram University will not graduate its first class for two more years, you have only three spaceports, most of your land is still undeveloped. Faligor has made extraordinary progress, but it is not yet ready to compete with the worlds of the Republic on an equal footing."

Bobby smiled. "Then you will help us."

"We *are* helping you, Your Majesty," said Cartright. "Faligor has made more progress than anyone had any right to expect. And it will continue to progress."

"Then we should be allowed to join the Republic, and progress under their watchful eye."

"You are progressing under their watchful eye already."

"It is not the same thing."

"Might I ask what has brought about this suddeninterest in joining the Republic?" interjected Beddoes. "This is the first any of us has heard of it."

Bobby shrugged. "I went to Sirius V to watch this man Billy Wycynski fight before offering to bring him here. Have you been to Sirius V, Arthur?"

"No."

"Susan?"

"Once, many years ago," she replied.

"It is a huge world," said Bobby. "Far bigger than Faligor. But it has a population of only thirty-five thousand, and *it* is a full member of the Republic."

"There are reasons," said Cartright.

"I would be pleased if you would tell me what they are."

"Sirius V was one of the very first planets colonized by Man when we went forth into the galaxy. It has been an important shipbuilding and mining world to us for more than a millennium. Furthermore, there are no native inhabitants on Sirius V; it is entirely a human colony."

"There *were* natives once," noted Bobby ironically.

"That is an unhappy moment in our history. We were terraforming the planet, and did not realize that they were sentient." Cartright paused uncomfortably. "At any rate, the entire population of Sirius V has been human for more than a thousand years now."

"Are you saying no world that is not predominantly human can join the Republic?" asked Bobby. "I happen to know that is not true."

"No, of course I am not saying that. We have made our mistakes in the past, but over the years we have recognized them and rectified most of them. There was a time when worlds were assimilated into the Republic against their will, but that time has thankfully passed. These days, a world must vote to become a member of the Republic."

"I am sure I can convince my people to vote for that."

"Your people are the Enkoti," replied Cartright. "The entire planet must vote for membership, and most of the people on this planet cannot yet read a ballot. Furthermore, the Republic strongly favors worlds with a planetary government, so they know who they will be dealing with. They don't want to contract for so many tons of grain from the Rizzali, only to find that war has broken out with the Traja and their fields have been burned.''

"These are all minor problems, capable of solution," said Bobby. "I suggest that you and I put our heads together and start solving them.''

"I repeat," said Cartright. "We *are* solving them, and at an unprecedented pace.''

"You see?" said Bobby with a smile. "We have faith in you, Arthur." He looked out across the lawn. "Excuse me for a moment. I see the Ambassador from Lodin XI has just arrived. Time for me to play the obsequious host.''

And with that, he arose and walked off to greet his newest guest.

"Well," said Cartright, and then repeated himself: "Well. What do you make of that?''

"You mean his going over to be 'obsequious' to the Lodinite ambassador?" asked Beddoes. "He's just trying to let you know that he's got alternatives. I hear that Lodin XI is about to join the new Association of Worlds that the Canphorites are organizing.''

"No," said Cartright impatiently. "I mean what did you think about the rest of what he said? He knows we can't take Faligor into the Republic for decades.''

"Of course he knows it, Arthur," said Beddoes.

"Then what was that all about?''

"I think it's obvious," she said. "He knows it's time to start preparing for membership, and he's putting in his bid."

"His bid?"

Beddoes smiled. "You've been dealing in huge problems and theoretical situations for too long. What we have here is a very practical, pragmatic one. You even said it yourself: before Faligor can join the Republic, it's got to have a planetary government. Right now, the Enkoti are the only tribe capable of governing Faligor. Ten or fifteen years from now that might not be so, so he wants to set up the government now."

Cartright frowned. "You're sure that's it?"

"Pretty sure." She paused and watched Emperor Bobby charming the Lodinite and his party. "He's no fool, Arthur. If you offered him full membership tomorrow, I think he'd turn it down. He's just angling for the best possible deal for his people."

"His people being the Enkoti?"

"He considers himself an Enkoti, not a Faligori, and his people have been the dominant tribe for centuries. He just wants to make sure they remain on top."

"Well," said Cartright after some consideration, "he does have a point. The Enkoti *are* the most politically sophisticated tribe on the planet." He paused. "Still, we've got to get them to start thinking of themselves as one people, instead of twenty or thirty different tribes."

"Arthur, they were living in huts less than a decade ago. How long did it take Men to forego their national identities and start thinking of themselves simply as Terrans?"

"We didn't have anyone to help us," answered Cartright defensively. "We had no examples to follow."

"Well," she said with a shrug, "you're the politician. I'm just an entomologist."

"You don't think it can be done?"

"I don't know," said Beddoes. "If you'd told me five years ago that we'd be sipping cognac at a lawn party hosted by a jason, I'd have said you were crazy. They're a remarkable race."

Cartright looked up. "And here comes the most remarkable of them to rejoin us."

Emperor Bobby made his way across the lawn, gladhanding one and all, and finally arrived at their table.

"Well," he said, taking a seat and signaling for another drink, "I hope you're enjoying yourselves."

"We are, Your Majesty," said Cartright. "We were just discussing the upcoming prizefight."

"Were you indeed?" asked Bobby with a smile that suggested he didn't believe a word of it. "And what are your conclusions?"

"I think your fighter is overmatched."

"It's possible," agreed Bobby. "Actually, I've never seen him fight, but I'm told that he has defeated everyone he's met."

"He hasn't met anyone like Wycynski," said Cartright.

"And do you agree with him, Susan?" asked Bobby.

"I have no opinion."

"Ah. You are not a boxing fan?"

"I've never seen any reason why two people should climb into a ring and try to knock each other senseless."

"But it's not just a matter of strength, but of skill," said Bobby. "The strongest doesn't always win. It is said that a good boxer will always defeat a good puncher. That means the intellect counts for something."

"Always assuming that it's still functioning after the first two blows to the head," responded Beddoes dryly.

Bobby threw back his head and laughed. "Men have such remarkable senses of humor! Is it any wonder that we cherish your company so?"

"Did I say something funny?"

"And such modesty!" added Bobby. "Susan, if you were a jason, I'd be inclined to propose marriage to you."

"Thank you for the compliment, Your Majesty," said Beddoes, "but you have six wives already, and my race practices monogamy."

"Isn't it Men who say that you can't have too much of a good thing?" asked Bobby, laughing uproariously at his own joke. He was about to say something else when suddenly a uniformed jason put a large Redbison horn to his lips and blew a few blaring notes through it. The assembled guests took their seats and fell silent.

"Ah!" said Bobby excitedly. "The entertainment!"

Billy Wycynski was the first to walk down the makeshift aisle between tables, nodding an occasional greeting to the four or five Men he recognized. His nose and left ear had been surgically reconstructed at various times during his career, but he was missing a number of teeth, and had evidently decided not to have them replaced until his career was over. It could have given him a silly grin, but for some reason the actual effect of his smile was one of ferocity. He was tall, well-muscled, and walked with a fluid grace. Once in the ring, his seconds removed his robe, and he danced lightly around, shadowboxing and trying to keep loose, as Bobby's human guests cheered and applauded.

A moment later Gama Labu, the Rizzali champion, emerged from his dressing tent, wearing a loose-fitting pair of knee-length shorts and disdaining a robe. Everything about him was big: his head, his neck, his shoulders, his chest, even his belly. His golden fur rippled with every step he took, and his small ears were in constant motion, listening to the comments of the audience as he passed by.

"You should have put him on a diet," remarked Cartright. "He's got to be forty pounds overweight."

"We expect great things of him," said Bobby. "Great things."

He stood and saluted as Labu moved past, and the fighter returned a slovenly salute and a huge grin.

"Well," said Bobby, trying to keep the contempt from his voice, "you can tell by that salute that he's not in the Enkoti army."

"He's a soldier?" asked Cartright.

"A minor officer, so I'm told."

Labu moved ponderously toward the ring. Beddoes could almost imagine the ground trembling beneath his feet, and the thought occurred to her that Emperor Bobby, all protests to the contrary, would not be heartbroken to see the champion of the Rizzali humbled in front of this assemblage. It was not an attitude that was shared by the other jasons in the audience, who roared their approval as Labu shuffled ponderously around the ring, trying to loosen his bulging muscles.

A human referee climbed into the ring, brought the fighters together for their last-minute instructions, then sent them to their corners. Wycynski kept dancing and shadowboxing, working up a mild sweat, while Labu simply stood in his corner, his arms draped over the ropes, smiling to some of his Rizzali tribal brothers in the crowd.

Then the bell rang, and Wycynski moved to the center of the ring, bobbing, weaving, jabbing, ducking. Labu seemed to approach him almost in slow motion, and threw a huge roundhouse right. The human segment of the audience gasped, then relaxed as Wycynski ducked it, stepped inside, and threw a flurry of six rights and lefts to the jason's midsection, then danced back out of reach with the Men's cheers ringing in his ears. Labu seemed more surprised than hurt, grinned foolishly at his opponent, and plodded after him. Each time he came within reach, Wycynski moved in quickly, delivered another flurry of punches, and withdrew before Labu could counter.

"They might as well stop it," said Cartright to Bobby. "Your fighter will be lucky to land a punch all night."

The sitate mumbled some answer, but never took his eyes from the ring.

Beddoes was watching the ring, too, and wondered if anyone else saw what she was seeing: that despite the fact that Wycynski was hitting him at will, Gama Labu seemed none the worse for all the punishment he was taking. He still had that foolish grin on his face, he still pursued his opponent doggedly if not gracefully, he seemed to feel no need to protect himself from the human champion's heaviest blows. And despite all the excess weight he was carrying, he wasn't puffing or gasping for air. *You may not look like much,* thought Beddoes, as the fighters returned to their corners amid much cheering from the humans and almost total silence from the jasons, *but you are one hell of a remarkable specimen.*

By the third round, Labu had convinced himself that his foe could do him no damage, and he walked out to the middle of the ring when the bell rang, spread his arms out, and invited Wycynski to take his best shot. The human looked surprised, but he wasted no time in accepting Labu's offer, and pummeled him for a full thirty seconds, stopping only when Labu broke out in peals of amused laughter, which was suddenly echoed by the jasons in the audience.

And suddenly the nature of the fight changed, for now Labu, who had still not landed a blow, began stalking Wycynski in earnest, and somehow, although he continued to move flat-footed, with his head down and his belly hanging over the elastic band of his shorts, Beddoes began to appreciate that he had a certain alien grace, that a Man moving like this might appear slovenly but that the jason seemed like an engine of destruction, bearing down relentlessly on his opponent. He cut off the ring, backed Wycynski into a corner, and moved in for what everyone in the crowd sensed would be the kill.

Wycynski was a champion, and he fought back like one, but the enormous jason merely shrugged off his blows and began pounding him, a right to the head, a left to the chest, a right to the jaw. With each punch, the jasons cheered wildly and the human's knees buckled more. Finally Labu turned to Emperor Bobby, and offered another clumsy salute, and the crowd, both jason and human, became suddenly silent. For just an instant Beddoes seemed to think he was staring directly at her and Cartright; then he grinned happily, turned back to his opponent, and delivered one final blow to the head. Wycynski collapsed, totally senseless, to the canvas. The jasons, except for Bobby, leaped to their feet as one, and applauded. A moment later, led by Cartright, the humans also stood up and clapped their approval, though less enthusiastically. Only the handful of moles, who seem to have taken little or no interest in the bout, remained seated.

After his hand had been raised in victory, Labu was given a microphone to address the crowd. It was announced that he spoke no Terran, and would use the Maringo dialect.

"I thank the Enkoti sitate for this opportunity," he said, flashing a huge smile at the crowd, and again Beddoes had the uneasy feeling he was looking in her direction. There was something about it that she found unnerving, something alien that she had never seen in Bobby or even Disanko. "It was fun."

And with that, he returned to his dressing room.

"Well, Susan," said Emperor Bobby, "now that you've seen a boxing match, what did you think of it?"

Beddoes paused for a moment. "I think Gama Labu has a curious sense of fun," she replied at last.

"Well, what can you expect from a Rizzali?" said Bobby with a deprecating shrug. He turned to Cartright. "Arthur, I should have bet you on the outcome."

"It was an impressive demonstration," replied Cartright.

"Perhaps we are closer to being your equals than you thought," suggested Bobby with a sly grin.

"Well, you certainly are in the boxing ring," agreed Cartright. "This Labu's like some kind of primal force."

"And outside the boxing ring?" persisted Bobby. "Have you given any thought to what we were discussing earlier?"

"Some," answered Cartright.

"And?"

"I suppose we should discuss it further."

"Excellent, my friend!" said Bobby, signaling a waiter. "Have another cognac."

"I don't mind if I do," said Cartright, holding out

his glass while the uniformed jason carefully filled it.

"And what shall we toast?" asked Bobby.

"That seems obvious," answered Cartright. "To Gama Labu. I expect to hear a lot more of him in the future."

"Oh, I'm sure you will," said Emperor Bobby.

I hope not, thought Beddoes.

Four

The Republic gave Faligor thirty years in which to raise its productivity and economy and literacy rate to the level at which it would be invited to join as a full member, following the necessary plebiscite among its inhabitants. Emperor Bobby thought it was far too long; Beddoes thought it was half a century too short; but Cartright, who had negotiated it with his superiors in the government, thought it was just about right, and so the decree came down.

Despite Bobby's impatience, a lot of work remained to be done to prepare Faligor for its entry into the Republic as a free and independent world, and first on the agenda was the formation of a planetary government. Given the literacy rate, an election would have been counterproductive, so Cartright, upon the advice of his aides, decreed that the Sitate Robert August Tantram II was the provisional president of the world. Free to form his own cabinet,

Bobby filled the sixteen positions with one member each of the Traja, the Rizzali, and the Bolimbo, and thirteen Enkoti.

It was at that point that Cartright intervened and insisted upon a more equitable distribution of political power. Bobby countered, not unreasonably, that if Cartright could find, for example, a Rizzali or a Traja who knew more about agricultural production or economics than his Secretaries of Agriculture and the Treasury, he would be happy to replace them. They laboriously went through a list compiled by the other tribes, and finally came up with a cabinet composed of ten Enkoti and six non-Enkoti.

This did not sit well with the other tribes, but then Cartright and Bobby made a joint pronouncement that within five years the cabinet would be representative of the population as a whole, and that in the meantime it was essential that the tribes send their best and their brightest to Tantram University in Romulus. And, since it had been decreed not only by the President, but even more importantly, by the Men who gave him his orders, they had no choice but to comply.

The next problem was the moles, which proved not to be a problem at all. Most of them had signed three and five-year contracts, and when the contracts were up, about half of them elected not to renew them, though most of them chose to remain on the planet, and many sent for their families (which, in mole society, could number up to fifty). At first Cartright feared that supporting them would put an unnecessary financial burden on the planet and cause resentment among the jasons, but the moles had no intention of not supporting themselves, or of competing with the jasons for various menial jobs. With the advent of a monied economy, there was an urgent need for shopkeepers, and the moles soon were entrenched as Faligor's merchant class, setting up shops in all the major population centers and even out in the hinterlands, importing goods not just from their own world but from many of the nearby worlds of the Republic, and indeed forming the tax base from which the planetary government drew most of its revenues. They were a serious, industrious race, and as the jasons, faced with the absence of a barter economy, began applying for work in the mines, more and more of the moles joined their brethren in the merchant sector.

As tourism boomed, the last few private hunting preserves were banned, and offworlders arrived with nothing but holographic cameras instead of weapons. The five major game reserves, run primarily by fanatically dedicated Men and assisted by jasons, soon began pulling business away from Peponi and even Serengeti. Luxury lodges accommodated the visitors, and it was said that there was no planet in the galaxy that could match the richness of Faligor's wildlife.

Bobby began spending more time on other worlds, ostensibly to solicit investment in Faligor, though he spent more time playing than working, but as Cartright noted, it was probably for the best, since it forced the government to function without him, and he had never been overly interested in the workings of government to begin with.

And, a handful of years after they left the planet for schooling within the Republic, a number of the jasons returned home. Most of them were Enkoti, but a few of them weren't, and of that few, the most brilliant of them was a middle-aged jason who had taken the human name of William to go with his tribal name of Barioke. He was a Rizzali, and unlike most of the others of his race, he had gone to school not on a human world, but rather on the world of Canphor VI. Over the millennia, the Canphorites had revolted three different times against human rule and were currently the leaders of a loosely-knit federation of nonhuman worlds that had ceased all intercourse with the Republic.

Whereas Emperor Bobby wanted nothing more than to join the Republic as a full partner, William Barioke wanted total independence from the Republic. He had no intention of turning down any aid the Republic might continue to give and he didn't want to break off relations with it, but he found the status of Protectorate to be demeaning, and the advantages of being a member world to be minimal. He had made contacts within the Canphorites, and saw no reason not to deal with both sides; he would let the Republic and the Canphor Federation bid for his loyalty (which, as he explained to his people, was never for sale, a fact that he felt would in no way inhibit the bidding).

The one thing on which Barioke and Bobby were in total agreement was that Men had totally underestimated their ability to handle their own affairs. Barioke saw no reason to allow Men to assist in the running of Faligor's affairs. After all, he argued, the ultimate goal of everyone involved, whether the planet became a member of the Republic or an independent entity, was self-rule, and the sooner it was begun the better. He lobbied the Rizzali, he lobbied the rest of the jasons, he lobbied the Men who lived and worked on the planet, he even lobbied the moles—but most of all, he lobbied Emperor Bobby.

Finally, Bobby agreed to make two public appearances with Barioke, in both of which he gave his approval to the notion of immediate self-rule, which was followed by Barioke's impassioned oratory. It was after the second rally that Beddoes requested an audience with him.

It took her a week to be ushered into his presence, since he had been spent the intervening days partying on nearby Beta Lemoris III, but finally she found herself sitting across a desk from the Emperor, who looked none the worse for wear for all the traveling he had done lately. From the paintings and holographs on the wall, the shape of the desk and chairs, the carpeting on the floor, she would never have guessed that she was in an alien's office had she not known otherwise.

"How nice to see you again, Susan," said Bobby, his golden fur rippling as he shot her an ingratiating smile. "How goes your insect collecting?"

I'll give you this: you're every inch a politician, she thought, not without a touch of admiration.

"Arthur Cartright has asked me to speak to you, Your Majesty," she replied.

"And how is my old friend Arthur doing?" he asked. "I haven't seen him for months."

"He's very busy these days," she replied. "We've opened up another dozen mining worlds this year."

"Tell him to come to Faligor for a vacation," suggested Bobby.

"Faligor is never far from his mind," answered Beddoes. "In fact, I'm here at his request."

"Ah," he said, and suddenly his face looked more like an unhappy puppy than a jason *or* a Man. "The speeches."

"He feels that you're giving your people expectations that cannot be realized," said Beddoes.

"Ever?" asked Bobby sharply.

"In the immediate future," said Beddoes. "Furthermore, you have aligned yourself with a very capable politician who has no desire whatsoever to join the Republic."

"He's just a Rizzali rabble-rouser," replied Bobby, with a shrug—unique to his species—that started at his cranium and slowly rippled his golden fleece all the way down to his three-toed feet.

"Then why associate with him?"

"Because he's a very popular rabble-rouser, and I am the President of *all* my people."

"He is very dangerous, Your Majesty," said Beddoes.

"I have every intention of assimilating him into my government, where he will be given some official function and never be heard from again," Bobby assured her. "But in the meantime, he and I happen to agree that things are moving too slowly. We really should not have to come to you, hat in hands, to beg for self-rule. We had it before you landed on our planet. We never gave it away, so why should we have to debase ourselves to get it back?"

"I fail to see how educating your people, expanding your economy, vaccinating your children, and showing you how best to make use of your natural resources constitutes debasement," said Beddoes.

"I don't doubt that you fail to see it," responded Bobby. "Probably this is because no one has ever given your race orders."

"Everything we have suggested—and we have *suggested*, not *ordered*—has been for Faligor's benefit, Your Majesty."

"Nevertheless, we resent being denied self-rule. On that point, Barioke and I think as one."

"It is possible that the length of time you remain a Protectorate can be shortened," said Beddoes, "but not if you ally yourself with Barioke."

"He is a very astute political thinker," said Bobby.

"He's too smart by half."

"He frightens you, does he?" asked Bobby, amused.

"Nothing frightens the Republic," answered Susan. "But he should frighten *you*, Your Majesty."

Bobby laughed again. "He is just a Rizzali."

"You know that the size of the Rizzali army has tripled since he returned from the Canphor system."

"All of the countries of Faligor have armies," said Bobby dismissively.

"Why?" asked Beddoes. "The jasons only own seven spaceships, and four of them are yours. What worlds do you plan to go to war with?"

"Let me assuage your doubts, Susan," said Bobby with a smile. "The armies are just for show, and to protect our territorial borders. As for the Rizzali army, it is a joke, commanded by the biggest clown of all."

"Prego Katora is no clown," Beddoes pointed out. "He graduated from one of the finest military academies on Deluros VIII."

"Prego Katora no longer commands the Rizzali army," answered Bobby.

"No?"

"Do you remember the boxing match I sponsored some time back?"

"Yes," said Beddoes warily. "What of it?"

"Do you remember Gama Labu, the jason who beat your champion?"

"Yes."

"Well, it is Labu, with the body of a self-indulgent giant and the intellect of a child, who is now in charge of Barioke's army." Bobby threw back his head and laughed. "Labu, who cannot even spell his name! If you were to tell him the enemy was gathering to the east, he would probably launch an attack on the Hills of Heaven. *Now* do you see why Barioke does not worry me?"

"I think you have more to fear than you realize, Your Majesty," said Beddoes sincerely.

"Because of Labu?" he said disbelievingly.

"There is something frightening about him," said Beddoes. "Something alien."

"Am *I* not an alien to you?" asked Bobby, amused.

"We are different species, but we hold certain basic principles in common. I think there is something about Gama Labu that is alien to all those things that we both cherish."

"And you base this on the fact that you saw him beat a human fighter in the ring?"

She shook her head. "No," she said slowly. "It is just a feeling I have about him."

"He is a clown," reasserted Bobby. "A great big clown. Always telling jokes, always drinking, always laughing loudest when he is the object of other people's jokes. He became a hero overnight when he defeated Billy Wycynski, and that doubtless caused his elevation to his current position, but nothing could be better for my purposes. In effect, it renders the Rizzali army useless. I will appropriate as much of William Barioke's support as I can, elevate him to a government position where I can control him, disband his army, and steer my people on a swift course that will culminate in self-rule."

"I think you are making a serious mistake, Your Majesty."

Bobby chuckled. "The day I can't control William Barioke is the day I'll retire from office and devote myself to a life of parties and sports."

I hope you'll tell us when it happens, so we'll know the difference, thought Beddoes caustically. Aloud, she said, "I cannot overstress the seriousness of the situation, Your Majesty."

"Certainly you can," said Bobby. "In fact, you already have."

"Arthur Cartright has empowered me to say that we will not support your alliance with Barioke, or your attempt to speed up the carefully-planned schedule for self-rule."

"Of course he'll support us," said Bobby. "Faligor is his noble experiment, the shining example upon which he has staked his reputation. How would it look if I toured the Republic complaining about the Department of Cartography's repression, or turned Gama Labu loose on your handful of military advisors, always assuming that he could find them?" Bobby grinned. "What would he do then, Susan? Call for the Navy he so despises to pacify us, as they have pacified so many other worlds?" He paused. "Arthur has his deadlines, and I have mine—and on my world, mine take precedence. I think Arthur had better get used to the idea that Faligor will be ruling itself within the next two years."

Beddoes stared at him silently, thinking about what she had heard.

"Come, come, Susan," he said easily. "Have you nothing to say?"

"I'm in an awkward position, Your Majesty," she replied. "I have delivered Arthur Cartright's message to you. To say anything further would be to exceed my authority." She paused, undecided. "And yet I have some things I very much want to say."

"I will consider all remarks to be confidential," answered Bobby.

She considered his offer for a moment, then sighed. "All right," she said. "You have us over a barrel, Your Majesty. Under no circumstances will Cartright call in the Navy. If you push for immediate self-rule hard enough, he'll have to agree to it."

"Your words will not leave my office," Bobby assured her. "No one will ever claim that Susan Beddoes was the first Man to yield to our demands."

She shook her head. "I don't care if *that* leaves your office or not. The truth of it is self-evident. You know and I know and Arthur knows that he won't use force against you."

"Then what is it you wished to say?" asked Bobby.

Beddoes again considered keeping silent, but finally decided to speak. "You are doubtless going to have a planetary vote on self-rule," she began.

"Certainly."

"And it will win overwhelmingly."

"I would assume so."

"Your first order of business will be to elect a planetary government," she continued, "and I assume you will be running for the Presidency."

"That is my intention," said Bobby.

"If there is any chance whatsoever that William Barioke will run against you," she said, staring directly into his eyes, "I think you should do everything in your power to see that such an eventuality does not come to pass."

"You make it sound positively sinister," said

Bobby, once again amused. "Would you care to define 'everything'?"

"I would not, Your Majesty. I would merely urge it."

Bobby got to his feet, signifying that the meeting was over.

"I am the acting President of Faligor, descended from three hundred sitates," he said, walking her to the ornate door of his office. "William Barioke is merely a Rizzali who I have chosen to use for my own political ends. Still," he added, "I thank you for your concern. When the election is over, I will remember who my friends are."

"I just hope you remember who your enemies are before the election is held," said Beddoes sincerely.

Five

The election was held twenty-two months later. The people of Faligor, as expected, voted overwhelmingly for self-rule.

Despite Cartography's opposition—or possibly because of it—William Barioke was elected President over Robert August Tantram II by a margin of 53 percent to 47 percent. As a gesture of goodwill and solidarity, the winner created the office of Prime Minister for the loser.

And Susan Beddoes took a long look at the rolling grassy plains outside her window and the fog-shrouded Hills of Heaven off in the distance, and decided that it was time to think of leaving the Diamond of the Outer Frontier and returning to the worlds of the Republic.

II

GLASS

Interlude

Y ou wander through the streets, past the ruins of the notorious Government Science Bureau, the smell of the dying and the dead heavy in the air. You can see the green savannah between the frames of two burnt-out houses, stretching all the way to the so-called Hills of Heaven, and you wonder if a single living thing exists anywhere within your field of vision.

It's difficult to remember that Johnny Ramsey once wandered those plains, hunting animals for the natural history museum back on Deluros VIII, that Sabare University was once considered the finest alien seat of learning on the Outer Frontier, that Men and jasons and moles lived and worked in peace and tranquility not fifty yards from where you are standing.

Oh, you've heard the stories, read the headlines, seen holographs of the slaughter—but that was all about some incredibly distant world gone mad. It had no relevance to you. Now you're here, and try as you might, you can't imagine how it came to pass.

Did no one see what was coming? Were no voices raised in protest? If the jasons didn't care, what about the thousands of Men who had made this their home? Wasn't there a day, an hour, a moment, when one of them could have stood up and said, "Stop! This far and no farther!"

And where was the Republic during this descent into hell? It opened the world, educated the people, taught them farming and mining and commerce and the complexities of government. How could it just turn its back and pretend nothing was happening?

Good questions, all. But the one you keep coming back to is this: How did it all begin? . . .

Six

There were problems right from the start.

Since Emperor Bobby had erected enough modern buildings in Romulus to house a government, William Barioke, rather than spending the money to build a new capital, simply appropriated Romulus for his own. Within a month of the election, the opera house had been converted into the Parliament, the theater into the High Court, the two largest tourist hotels into government offices, and Bobby's own house became the Presidential Mansion.

Soon Romulus, which had been populated almost exclusively by Men and the Enkoti, was overrun with members of the Rizzali, most of whom were working for the government. Bobby protested to Arthur Cartright, who explained that the emperor had insisted on self-rule and would now have to live with the consequences of his actions.

After a few months of lobbying without success, Bobby decided to move the Prime Minister's offices to Remus, some fifty miles away. He paid for a new mansion with his own funds, but managed to raise the money for a new theater and sports complex from Men and moles, and within less than a year Remus had replaced Romulus as the cultural center of Faligor, and most of the commerce moved there as well.

As the Men and moles followed the Enkotis' exodus from Romulus, the capital began falling into a state of disrepair. Barioke spent a fruitless three months urging them to move back, and then appropriated Remus for the government as well.

Bobby, who understood how government worked, went to the press and vehemently protested—but Barioke, who understood how *power* worked, simply shut down those segments of the media that presented the prime minister's case. Then the president took to the airwaves—everywhere but in the heartland of the Enkoti—and explained that he was the president of *all* the jasons, and that he would never agree to the Enkoti demand for special treatment. If the prime minister would not abide by the constitution, he concluded, then he would reluctantly have to remove him from office.

Bobby countered by holding a huge rally at the recently-constructed sports arena in Remus. Forty thousand Enkoti and Men filled the seats, and after a few lesser Enkoti officials addressed the crowd, Bobby himself stood before the microphones.

''I will not stand by and watch my people being

systematically robbed by a government that has sworn to eradicate tribalism and favoritism," he announced. "Where in the constitution does it say that entire cities can be appropriated by executive fiat or, even worse, by executive whim? Where does it say that the president can deny the prime minister access to the media? The Enkoti don't ask for special treatment, but merely for *fair* treatment—and if we cannot get it from William Barioke, then we shall present our case to the Republic."

During the applause that followed, Bobby scanned the faces at the front of the audience, and stopped when he came to a huge jason in a military uniform.

"I see that Barioke has sent his general here to listen to what I have to say," he continued. "And doubtless to report every word back to him." He paused and smiled. "Are the words I'm using too big for you, General Labu?" he asked sarcastically.

The audience laughed, none more loudly than Gama Labu himself.

"Perhaps you would like to come up onto the platform and tell us what you are doing here?" said Bobby.

Labu, accompanied by his own personal translator, got to his feet and climbed the small set of stairs with his ungainly stride.

"I am not political," he said, speaking in Maringo and obviously uncomfortable before such a large audience. "We are all jasons, and I will never hold a grudge against another of my kind. I am a soldier, so I go where my president sends me, but I have no opinion in these matters."

"And what will you tell your president?" demanded Bobby when the translator had finished.

Labu grinned. "That the arena food is not very good, but the human beer is excellent!"

The tension was diffused by a burst of laughter. Labu smiled and waved to the crowd, then took his seat and listened as Bobby concluded his tirade.

The next morning Labu was back, with five hundred soldiers, to place the prime minister under house arrest.

The first person Bobby sent for was Arthur Cartright, who showed up half an hour later and found his way blocked by Labu himself.

"What is the meaning of this?" demanded Cartright. "I have been summoned here by the prime minister."

Labu shrugged, a grotesque gesture for an alien with his enormous bulk.

"Thank you very much," he said with a smile.

"I beg your pardon?"

"Thank you very much," repeated Labu.

Then Cartright remembered that the jason did not speak Terran, and he switched to the Maringo dialect.

"What is going on here?" he said.

"I am simply following my orders," replied Labu.

"You were ordered to arrest the prime minister and confine him to his house?" said Cartright. "Why?"

Labu shrugged again. "I have no idea," he said. "I am sure it must be a mistake, and will soon be corrected."

"Does the president know about this?"

"He is the one who issued the order," replied Labu with a huge grin.

Cartright paused and stared at Labu for a moment. "The prime minister has sent for me," he said at last. "May I please pass through your lines?"

"Of course, friend Cartright," said Labu. "We are great friends, are we not?"

"I don't know," said Cartright. "Are we?"

"Of course, of course," said Labu, thumping him on the back. "I have no enemies."

"That must be a great comfort," said Cartright.

Labu laughed uproariously, as if Cartright had just made a joke, then stepped aside and signaled his men to let the human through. A moment later another uniformed jason escorted him into the mansion and up to the door of Bobby's bedroom. The door slid open long enough for Cartright to step inside the room, then closed behind him.

"Arthur!" said Bobby, rising from a huge desk where he had been scribbling something in longhand. "I am so glad you came!"

"What's happened?" asked Cartright. "I got your message, and I arrived to find your house surrounded by the army."

"I don't know!" said Bobby. "They haven't charged me with anything—but they won't let me leave!"

"Last night's speech didn't exactly endear you to your enemies," said Certright. "Let me contact Barioke and see what we can work out."

"Thank you."

Cartright left the prime minister's home and returned to his office, where he called Barioke on the
vidphone. After twenty minutes of being transferred
from one bureaucrat to another, he was finally con-
nected to the lean, conservatively-attired president.

"Good morning, Mr. Cartright," said Barioke.
"I've been expecting to hear from you."

"Then you must know why I'm calling, Mr. President."

"Certainly."

There was a long pause.

"Well?" said Cartright.

"Well what, Mr. Cartright?"

"Why has he been arrested?"

"He has not been arrested," replied Barioke. "No
charges have been made."

"Then why has he been confined to his quarters by
the head of your army?"

"Because I don't know what to do with him, and
I am keeping him there until I can decide."

"That's illegal!"

"Would you be happier if I charge him with treason?" asked Barioke mildly. "I have every right to,
you know."

"He's broken no laws."

"He threatened to disobey a presidential edict,"
said Barioke, "and he did it in front of forty thousand witnesses. Left to his own devices, I am sure he
will eventually urge the Enkoti to rebel against the
planetary government and set up their own separate
state."

"You can't arrest him because of what you think he *might* do!" said Cartright.

"Do you think it would be wiser to wait until he has completely discredited the duly elected government?" asked Barioke sardonically.

"I think the two of you should get together and sort out your differences," said Cartright. "I will be happy to act as a mediator if you feel one is necessary."

"I think not," said Barioke. He paused and turned his piercing eyes full upon Cartright's image in his vidscreen. "Let us understand one another, Mr. Cartright. *You* are the one who did not wish my planet to obtain self-rule for another quarter of a century. You are the one who has constantly favored the Enkoti in all things. You are the one who made that irresponsible, game-playing spendthrift the interim president. You are the one who urged your fellow Men to erect their buildings and start their businesses on Enkoti land. And now you are urging me to deal with an Enkoti who has publicly condemned my government. You are not my friend, Mr. Cartright. I am trying to unify this world, and you are hindering me every bit as much as the prime minister, perhaps more."

"That is a very one-sided statement of the facts," responded Cartright. "Robert August Tantram was elected prime minister by your people, not mine."

"In point of fact, he was defeated by my people, and appointed to a meaningless office by *me*," said Barioke. "In retrospect, it was a mistake. He has opposed me at every turn."

"He has only requested that you not appropriate the private property of the Enkoti for governmental use."

"He does not request; he demands. And I should point out that the prime minister and his tribe possessed the property we have confiscated only because of the favored treatment his father and brother received at the hands of your race. You literally threw money at them, Mr. Cartright. They did nothing to earn it, except to give you a free hand to use our world as your Department's grand social experiment."

"I resent the implication!" said Cartright. "We have helped elevate *all* the jasons. Our medical clinics have been constructed in every tribal homeland, our teachers have gone into the most remote areas, our—"

"But always you have begun with the Enkoti," interrupted Barioke. "You make it sound as if I wish to enslave them, Mr. Cartright. All I wish to do is redress the inequities and unify all the inhabitants of Faligor. No Enkoti will suffer during my rule."

"What kind of impression do you think you're making on the Enkoti right now, with hundreds of soldiers surrounding the prime minister's residence?"

"A momentary disruption, nothing more," said Barioke. "If he will publicly apologize for attacking the government and swear fealty to it, all will be forgiven."

"And if not?"

"Then I shall have to charge him with treason."

"That's ridiculous!" snapped Cartright.

"I realize that you and I have honest disagreements, Mr. Cartright," said Barioke, "but I cannot permit you to address me like that."

"I apologize, Mr. President," said Cartright, struggling to control his temper. "But I helped draft your constitution. It guarantees freedom of speech, and all that the prime minister did last night was exercise that right."

"I have studied your laws, Mr. Cartright," said Barioke, still unperturbed, "and I think you and I both know that freedom of speech is not an absolute, that there are circumstances under which it can and indeed must be restricted."

"Voicing an honest opinion about the government is not one of them."

"And if it is his honest opinion that the government must be overthrown by force, or that the Enkoti must secede, is *that* protected by our constitution?"

"He did not urge anyone to secede or use force," said Cartright. "I was there."

"There were nuances and implications," answered Barioke.

"You don't charge someone with treason because of nuances."

"This is getting us nowhere, Mr. Cartright," said Barioke. "If you will give me your word that he will make no further public statements, the army will withdraw immediately and his freedom will be restored."

"Let me speak to him."

"Certainly," replied Barioke. A small smile

crossed his face. "He is not, after all, going anywhere."

Cartright broke the connection and immediately
called Bobby.

"What did Barioke say?" asked Bobby the moment he looked at his screen and saw that he was
speaking to Cartright.

"He says that if you'll promise not to criticize the
government again, he won't press any charges."

"And the army?"

"They'll withdraw."

"We've created a tyrant, Arthur. The Republic has
to do something about him."

"I don't know exactly what the Republic *can* do,"
replied Cartright. "You're no longer a Protectorate,
and you're not yet a member. You're an independent
world."

"You've got to get them to apply economic pres-
sure," continued Bobby. "If he can do this to me, he
can do it to anyone who speaks out. He's not always
going to have Gama Labu in charge of the army; the
next commander could be a serious threat to the
populace." He paused. "Why is he doing this, Arthur?"

"He has his reasons," answered Cartright. "I
don't think they're valid, but I'm willing to believe
that *he* does. I think the best thing to do is to try to
set up a meeting between the two of you."

"Do you think he'll do it?"

"Not if you don't promise to stop criticizing him
in public."

Bobby lowered his head in thought for a moment,

then looked up and bared his teeth in a very alien grin. "Tell him he's got a deal."

"I mean it," said Cartright. "And more to the point, *he* means it. If you speak out against him again, I can't protect you."

"I won't say anything against him," answered Bobby. "You have my word on that."

"All right," said Cartright. "I'll call him and tell him you've agreed to his terms, then see what I can do about arranging a meeting."

Two hours later Bobby was freed.

Four days later, President William Barioke refused to meet with him.

One week later, Bobby gave another speech. This time he never mentioned Barioke by name, but made an impassioned argument that it was time for Faligor to apply for full membership in the Republic, that only the Republic could assure that no tyrant ever ruled the planet, and that he himself planned to travel to the Deluros system to present his case.

The next morning, Gama Labu led his five hundred men down the streets of Remus toward Bobby's home. When they got within three hundred yards, they were met by gunfire from an army of two thousand Enkoti warriors.

Labu retreated half a mile, sent for reinforcements, joked with the press and onlookers while awaiting them, explained once more that he was simply a soldier carrying out his orders and that the politics of the situation were beyond him, and then stormed the mansion.

Twenty minutes later Robert August Tantram II,

the 302nd sitate of the Enkoti, and two thousand of his followers, lay dead in the ashes of his mansion. Before sunset, they were buried outside of town in a mass grave.

That evening William Barioke announced that the constitution would be suspended for a period of three months, while a better document, one that would never allow a traitor to rise to the rank of prime minister, was drafted and implemented.

And Arthur Cartright sat by his video, listening to the news and wondering what he could have done differently, and trying to determine exactly what had gone wrong.

Seven

" "Has he written the last chapter yet?"
That was the joke among the Men who lived on Faligor, and it referred to the constitution which William Barioke had suspended for three months. But the more he tinkered with it, the less he liked the results, and three years later the constitution was still being rewritten.

Barioke decided that there was no need to allow the office of prime minister to remain vacant, simply because there was no constitution, so he combined it with the office of president. And since there was no constitution to state how elections should be held, there were no elections.

General Labu went on video a week after the death of Emperor Bobby to apologize to the public; he assured them that he had no grudge against the Enkoti, and was merely following his orders. He deeply regretted the fact that he been forced to kill so many of

Bobby's followers to protect his own men, and he assured anyone who was listening that he was just a soldier who had sworn his loyalty to the president, even when he didn't necessarily agree with the president's orders.

Barioke considered firing him for insubordination, but found that the speech had made Labu an overnight hero, and any action taken against the huge soldier might well result in an insurrection. So instead the president called his general to his office, they hugged each other for the holo cameras, and another crisis was averted.

Things remained calm for a few months, and then disconcerting rumors began to reach Remus: the Bolimbo had tortured and killed two members of the Traja, the Rizzali had set fire to the home of an Enkoti merchant who had opened a business in one of their cities, the Enkoti refused to trade with the Bolimbo. Sabare University, which was dominated by Enkoti, refused admission to three qualified Rizzali students in retaliation for the burning of the Enkoti home. More than twenty thousand moles, assuming they would be the next group to be discriminated against, emigrated back to their home planet.

Finally Cartright organized a group of some dozen Men and gained an audience with Barioke.

Your society, explained the Men, is falling apart. Something must be done to combat this re-emergence of tribalism. You are the president. If you won't ratify a new constitution, at least do something about this problem, or before long Faligor will need twenty-seven constitutions, one for each tribe.

Barioke heard them out, pledged to attack the problem with all the forces at his command, and thanked them for this show of concern. They left his office half-convinced that he really meant to take some action.

But no one was quite prepared for the action he took.

Within two weeks he had nationalized all the mines, and before three months had passed, the government had assumed ownership of all businesses that employed more than one hundred jasons.

With each acquisition, Barioke went on the video to explain his actions: the best way to combat tribalism was to totally remove it from the economy. Jasons no longer worked for Enkoti or Rizzali or Traja employers, but for the government, which was not a tribe, but rather a combination of *all* the tribes.

There were cries of outrage from those jasons whose businesses had been appropriated, but the cries grew fewer and farther apart after Barioke had the apologetic Labu march his army through the streets in front of the establishments in question.

Since the government did not pay taxes to itself, the assimilation of all the major industries made a major dent in the tax base, and Barioke's answer was to raise taxes on all other segments of the planet's economy. Since the Enkoti had the most to give, they were taxed at the highest rate; his own Rizzali were taxed at the lowest, and could avoid all taxes whatsoever simply by having a member of their immediate family serving in the military.

Complaining to the government was useless, to say nothing of dangerous, and numerous committees of jasons visited Cartright and the other Men who were stationed in Remus, imploring them to intervene with Barioke on their behalf.

Finally Cartright yielded to their pleas and arranged another meeting between himself, a handful of his aides, and Barioke.

"Mr. President," said Cartright, when the men had been ushered into a large meeting room in the presidential palace, "this is not what we had in mind when we warned you about tribalism."

"Have there been any outbreaks of tribalism lately?" asked Barioke calmly.

"Yes," said Jeffrey Samuels, a former naval commander who had retired to a huge farm about thirty miles south of Romulus.

"Oh?" said Barioke. "And who is the guilty party?"

"The government, sir," said Samuels.

"Mr. Samuels, if you were a jason, I could have you executed for making such a statement," said Barioke without raising his voice. "As you are a Man, I shall overlook it." He paused and stared at Samuels. "This one time."

"And since you are not a Man, I shall overlook your threat this one time," shot back Samuels.

"Gentlemen, this meeting is over," said Barioke. "You are guests of Faligor, and if you will not behave as guests, I will not listen to you."

"Please, Mr. President," said Cartright hastily. "I am sure Mr. Samuels meant no offense. It is essential that this meeting take place. We have only Faligor's best interests at heart.''

''Did you mean to offend, Mr. Samuels?'' asked Barioke.

Samuels glared at Cartright for a moment, then shook his head. ''No, I did not, Mr. President.''

''And if you knew you had caused offense, you would certainly apologize, would you not?'' continued Barioke.

''I apologize,'' said Samuels softly.

''Very well, then,'' said the president. ''Now, Mr. Cartright, what have you come to discuss?''

''Mr. President, this world has been without a constitution or an election for too long. The rights of the citizenry are being eroded almost daily. We cannot force you to change, but we strongly urge that you consider the consequences of your actions.''

''The consequences are quite clear,'' replied Barioke. ''Where there was tribalism, now there is none. Where there was unrest, now the cities are quiet. Where there was inequity, now there is equality.''

''Do you really believe that?'' demanded Samuels.

''You have made us a society of laws,'' responded Barioke. ''If you can show me a place where they are being broken, I will order the army there immediately to set matters right.''

Samuels got to his feet. ''He has no intention of listening to us, Arthur, and I, for one, am not going to waste my breath talking to him. We're going to have to get the Republic involved in this.''

He walked out the door, and Cartright was left to apologize for his behavior and steer the conversation

back on track. Barioke listened patiently for almost
two hours, made an occasional comment, thanked
the Men for their concern, and finally dismissed
them.

That evening Jeffrey Samuels was found dead behind a human restaurant in Romulus. The police
ruled it an attack by an unknown assailant, and released evidence to indicate that the murderer was a
mole. The next morning a mole shopkeeper was arrested, charged with the murder, and executed
before noon without a trial, while Samuels' family
received a note of condolence personally signed by
the president.

Cartright decided that Barioke had to be stopped,
and contacted those officials within the Republic
with whom he had remained in touch. Most ex-
pressed regret that they were unable to help him,
since Faligor was neither a Protectorate nor a member world; a few were genuinely amused that his
carefully-constructed utopia was falling apart and he
had to beg them for help. But whether amused or
regretful, the result was the same: Faligor would
have to solve its problems on its own.

Within weeks a jason journalist released a story
that Barioke had funneled millions of credits into a
private account on the nearby world of Talisman. He
was arrested that afternoon, but not before evidence
of his story was mailed to hundreds of Men and
government officials.

Barioke went on video two nights later to deny the
charges, declared that any story impugning the in-
tegrity of the office of the president or its present

occupant was an act of treason, and declared the matter closed. Nevertheless, a trio of Enkoti lawyers went to Talisman the next morning to institute proceedings to freeze Barioke's bank account until it could be determined whether the money had been misappropriated. As soon as word of their efforts reached him, Barioke flew to Talisman to defend his ownership of the funds.

And that evening, a large, round, familiar, fur-covered face appeared on every video channel.

"Good evening, citizens," it said in the Maringo dialect. "I have an announcement to make that is of major importance to every inhabitant of Faligor, no matter what his tribe or race." Gama Labu paused and smiled into the cameras. "As of sunset this evening, the army has taken temporary control of the government, and I will be the acting president until the constitution has been restored and we can once again hold free elections. William Barioke broke his covenant with the people of Faligor, and will face criminal charges if he returns to the planet."

Labu waited for the import of his statements to sink in, then continued: "The long dark era of tyranny and repression has ended. Never again will one tribe be favored over another. Never again will you have cause to fear your government. As a first step toward planetary unity, I have ordered that the body of the late prime minister, Robert August Tantram II, be exhumed and reunited with his ancestors in the Enkoti city of Romulus."

There were cheers from behind the camera, and Cartright, watching from his home, realized for the first time that Labu was addressing a live audience as well as an electronic one.

"I am only a soldier," he concluded. "My pleasures are few and simple. Most of you who know me"—he grinned self-consciously—"will attest to that. I have neither the training nor the desire to rule Faligor. I repeat: the military will step aside as soon as the new constitution goes into effect and we can hold elections. The darkness is about to end; tomorrow Faligor will shine in the sunlight once more."

Well, who ever would have thought that a fat clown would be Faligor's savior? mused Cartright. Yet maybe, just maybe, it could once again become the Diamond of the Outer Frontier.

Eight

Dear Susan:
   I'm sorry it has been so long since I've written to you, but things have been rather hectic here. It's spring-time and the flowers are blooming, everything has become green again after the long rains, and as I write this avians are singing just outside my window, but nevertheless I am afraid you would no longer recognize our beloved Faligor.

   I know you must be following the events here with much interest, but since the press is under as much control as all other aspects of life on this planet, I thought I would write you while the mail service is still functional. I apologize for not answering your last two subspace messages, but since I cannot be sure who might be monitoring my replies I thought it best to go back to the old tried-and-true method of putting pen to paper.

   It appears that you were right and I was wrong about President Labu. But of course, you must know that by now. If the press is reporting one-tenth of what he's done here, you must wonder why any of us have stayed on.

I'll grant him this: he fooled us all at first. The old bread-and-circuses routine. He was a big, bumbling friendly clown who seemed to go out of his way to be the butt of every joke, and to always shrug the laughter off good-naturedly. He did indeed disinter poor old Bobby and bury him with his ancestors. It was only some months later that I found out that what I just wrote was the literal truth: all 302 Enkoti sitates are now buried beneath the ground.

Still, Labu sponsored enormous public festivals during his first three months in office. He not only befriended any officials from the Republic that he could entice to his mansion, but also the Canphorites, the Lodinites, and every other alien race that he thought might be willing to give him money and arms to maintain his independence from the Republic.

Even when it became apparent that he was not the buffoon he seemed, his methods were so transparent that no one thought him a serious threat. You remember that holograph that appeared all over the Republic? Let me tell you how it came to pass.

Labu had some of his officials circulate rumors that the Republic was trying to manipulate his administration, and that we were urging him to erect trade barriers against all non-Republic worlds. This, of course, was totally false, but it's just the kind of thing the Canphorites would believe, and they complained bitterly about it. Labu invited them to take the matter up with his few remaining human advisors, who assured the Canphorites that these were malicious lies, and that no one was attempting to influence how Labu ran his government. The Canphorites, of course, demanded proof, and Labu suggested that a public display of his unquestioned authority would solve the problem.

He's a sly devil, and he hit upon a demonstration that would publicly humiliate us, which is why you saw the holo of six elderly humans, all in formal dress, carrying Labu in a sedan chair up to the podium from which he made his speech asserting that no one but Gama Labu ruled Faligor. Had they known just how long he would carry on about it, I doubt that any of the six men in question would have participated, but they thought they were pouring water on a fire. (Labu has this remarkable and hitherto unguessed-at capacity of turning water into oil.)

Then there was the Massacre. Again, it began simply enough. A number of Labu's thugs robbed some of the moles' shops in Romulus, and then hit Remus the next week. The moles and the Enkoti protested, and Labu used those protests as a pretext for declaring martial law in the twin cities, tripling the military presence there, and issuing an order that effectively suspended all civil rights: anyone suspected of being a thief was to be shot on sight, or incarcerated without a trial.

At first the Enkoti were willing to put up with this, since the streets were literally not safe to walk in—but then Labu's soldiers started shooting any Enkoti caught walking after dark. Also, hundreds of moles were imprisoned, and their shops were taken over by Labu's thugs.

And then came the night when something like seven hundred Enkoti held a torchlight parade to the spot where the sitates had been buried, to pay homage to them, and Labu's thugs killed every last one of them.

I realize I keep using the word "thug," which is a

generic term, but these are generic enforcers. Labu has gathered the discontented, the lawless, and the power-hungry about him without regard to tribe (except that none of them are Enkoti), has drafted them into the army, and has systematically used them to loot Enkoti farms and businesses.

Then there is the matter of Colonel George Witherspoon. If you haven't heard of him yet, you soon will.

Witherspoon is a gifted soldier, yet he was demoted three times during his career in the Republic's army: once for cruelty to soldiers serving under him, once for refusing to obey a direct order, and once for lying under oath during a friend's court martial. About eight years ago he was cashiered out of the service; it had something to do with a rape and murder that never came to trial. Since then he has wandered the Rim, the Spiral Arm, and the Inner Frontier as a mercenary, usually in the service of alien armies.

Somehow he came to Labu's attention, the two hit it off, and though he holds no official military title and is merely listed as one of Labu's many advisors, he has quickly become the second most powerful being on the planet. He is the one who determines what arms the military will buy, how best to deploy the army to prevent insurrection, which planetary governments to placate and which to ignore. It's rumored that he's also building a space fleet, and that he has acquired some thirty ships already.

And how, I hear you ask, can an undeveloped agricultural world pay for such things?

Well, first of all, Labu has kept control of the mines—and woe betide the jason who isn't willing to work in them when ordered to. That provides Gama Labu with the bulk of his hard currency.

Also, he has been charging missionaries of all races and religions exorbitant fees to set up shop here, which most of them have been willing to pay.

But his greatest source of funding comes from his own Treasury. An economics student who has since emigrated to Spica II told me that when the Treasury Secretary informed Labu that there wasn't enough money to pay for all the military hardware he wanted, Labu fired him and hired the first jason who agreed to keep the mint churning out money around the clock. So now Labu has his toys, but the average price for a canister of beer has risen from just two credits to three thousand four hundred in less than three months, and the price of meat went up even more. So along with everything else, we seem to be facing hyperinflation.

All that you probably know. It is a matter of record.

What follows is not recorded anywhere, and probably never will be. I cannot confirm most of it first-hand, but there are too many stories, too many missing people, for it to be totally false.

I said that Labu "fired" his Treasury Secretary, and that is the official story. Yet three different jasons I know have told me that Labu personally decapitated him after subjecting him to three days of torture. I asked them how they knew. Two simply stopped talking about it and changed the subject; the third tells me that he saw the decapitated head in the refrigerator of Labu's mansion.

Then there is the Government Science Bureau. I don't know what its original purpose was, since it was a gift of Bobby's to Romulus after we'd set him up as president. I assume it carried on various experiments dealing with agriculture and mining, but for all I know it was intended for medical research on laboratory animals.

I don't know what its current purpose is, but I can make a guess, because I was in Romulus one night last week on business, and I heard the most hideous screams coming from the upper levels. I immediately went by to see what was causing the commotion, but the military was stationed at all the doors and wouldn't let me in.

I have been told, though I haven't seen it with my own eyes, that a huge truck pulls up to the rear of the building each day. No one sees what it carts away, but the stench is said to be awful.

There is still no constitution, of course, and while Labu publicly encourages debate, those who take him up on it tend to vanish and are never seen again.

I don't know how it all happened, Susan. We studied the mistakes of our colonial ventures and tried to correct them. We kept the military out. We did nothing that could possibly offend the jasons. We not only gave them health care and modern agriculture methods, we set up mines that have virtually supported the entire planet. If we favored the Enkoti, we made it clear that it was only temporary, until the rest of the world caught up with them. We helped them draft a constitution that would serve as a model for any world in the galaxy.

And yet, since they achieved independence and self-rule, Faligor has had only two presidents, one a tyrant and the other a madman. The people voted in the first, and welcomed the second as if he were a hero come to liberate them.

And suddenly, in one short decade, Faligor has ceased to be a noble experiment, and has become instead a police state run by a ruler who can neither read nor write.

How did it come to this? Am I to blame? And if so, what did I do wrong?

And, more to the point, how can I make it right again?

So far Labu has been very circumspect in his treatment of humans, but none of us think that it will last, even with the unspoken threat of reprisal by the Republic. Witherspoon has convinced him that the Republic will never interfere with events on Faligor, and I have a sinking feeling that he is right. We lobbied so long and so hard for them to leave the development of Faligor in our hands, I think they will stay away, even if Men start feeling the brunt of Labu's madness, simply to prove a point to future social architects: if you don't want the military at the start, don't expect it to come in and rescue you after you've made a mess of things.

Still we remain, living our lives day by day, hoping that the madman will come to his senses and fearful that he will not. Each day brings some new abuse, some new barbarism, some hideous rumor made all the more hideous by the fact that we cannot disprove it, and yet we remain here. I don't think anyone believes it will be Johnny Ramsey's "Diamond of the Outer Frontier" anytime soon, but somehow or other we've got to put Faligor on the right track once again.

I think what keeps us here, those of us who haven't left, is our love of the jasons. They are such decent people, with such potential. They have no idea how to combat something like Gama Labu, and so we must do it for them, or at least show them the way. I still have difficulty believing that a Labu, or even a Barioke, could come from the same race that gave us a Disanko or even an ineffective but lovable ruler like Bobby.

I know I'm rambling, Susan, but it's not safe to say these things aloud. You never know who might be listening, and who might report you to Labu's thugs for money, for position, or—more likely—for the release of a loved one from the hundreds of prisons that have sprung up like weeds across the countryside.

I don't wish to unduly disturb you, but this may be the last letter I am able to write. Oh, not that anything will happen to me personally . . . but there is daily talk that offplanet mail service may be shut down, at least until Labu can set up a screening board to censor our letters. That's likely to take him a lifetime and then some, so few of his followers can read. The problem is that those who can read, and think for themselves, are not inclined to share their thoughts, at least not publicly—nor can I bring myself to blame them, since here I am, locked in my room with the windows covered, writing to someone who cannot possibly do anything about the situation.

I think about you often, and I miss you, as do we all. But this must not be construed as a plea for help, or for you to return. It's our problem, and we'll solve it. As for you, you're much better off where you are, and I hope by now you've found an insect bald and rotund enough to be named after me.

Love,
Arthur

Nine

The morning after Arthur Cartright wrote his letter to Susan Beddoes, a squadron of armed, uniformed jasons came to his house and placed him under arrest. Within an hour he had been taken to the jail in Remus, holographed, fingerprinted, retinagrammed, and placed in a cell. His demands to know why he was being incarcerated went unheeded.

His cell was eight feet by six feet, with a small bucket in the corner. There was a single barred window, from which he could look out over the main square of the city. There were no beds or cots, but he was given a pair of blankets so that he wouldn't have to sleep on the damp stone floor.

He spent three days alone in the cell. Each evening he was given a single plate of food that he could not identify and a cup of water. Each morning the plate and cup were removed and a fresh bucket placed in the corner. Whenever a guard passed by he asked if his lawyer had been informed that he had been imprisoned, but he received no answer.

On the morning of the fourth day, the door was opened, the plate and cup picked up, the bucket replaced, and then a badly-beaten jason was tossed roughly onto the floor of the cell. Before Cartright could ask any questions, the door was locked once again.

Cartright examined the jason, whose golden fleece was streaked with dried blood, and tried his best to make his new cellmate comfortable. There was no water with which to wash out the wounds, no bed on which to lay him, but he wrapped him in both blankets and, taking off his shirt, rolled it into a ball and used it as a pillow beneath the jason's head.

"Thank you," whispered the jason through bruised and bloodied lips. "You are Arthur Cartright, are you not?"

Cartright nodded. "Don't talk now. Just rest and try to regain some of your strength."

"For what purpose?" asked the jason. "We are doomed, you and I."

Cartright stared at the jason. "Don't I know you?" he said at last.

"We have met before," answered the jason. "I am the Reverend James Oglipsi."

"My God!" muttered Cartright. "If there was one jason I thought they'd be afraid to touch, it was you!"

"Why?" asked Oglipsi. "Because I am a Christian?"

"Because you've been standing up to Labu since the day he took office," said Cartright.

"Evidently I stood up to him once too often."

"He'll never get away with it!" said Cartright. "You've got tens of thousands of followers."

"He has already gotten away with it, Arthur Cartright. I am here, am I not?"

"But you've got all those devoted followers . . ." said Cartright.

"Who have been taught to turn the other cheek," answered Oglipsi wryly. "If I have done my job properly, then they will not try to free me or stand up to Labu. And if I have not, then I have failed and I might just as well die here as anywhere else."

"How did this happen?" asked Cartright. "You have been publicly denouncing him for half a year. Why did he arrest you *now?*"

"Two men from a nearby village were digging a well, when they came upon a dead body. The jasons do not bury their dead in unmarked graves, so the men dug further and discovered that they had unearthed a mass grave for more than two hundred corpses. The bodies had deteriorated beyond our ability to identify them individually, but we found several tokens of the Enkoti." The jason paused to catch his breath. "That was three . . . no, four . . . days ago. Yesterday morning I left my church and took my parishioners to the grave to pray for the souls of the poor butchered corpses. Colonel Witherspoon showed up with perhaps one hundred armed men, accused me of killing those people for supporting Gama Labu, and arrested me."

"And no one spoke up for you?" asked Cartright.

"The first forty to protest on my behalf were also arrested. The next handful were shot. After that, nobody said anything."

"But they know you're here!"

"These are farmers and peasants that I have converted to a religion of gentleness," said Oglipsi, shifting his position and trying unsuccessfully to get comfortable. "Surely you do not expect them to storm the jail and free me?"

"No," admitted Cartright. "No, I suppose not."

"Might I ask why you are here?" continued Oglipsi. "President Labu has usually gone out of his way not to offend the Republic."

"I'm not the Republic. I'm just a citizen of Faligor."

"But you are a Man, and the Republic protects Men wherever they may be."

"Not this time, Reverend," said Cartright. "First, they don't know I've been incarcerated. And second, even if they knew it, they wouldn't lift a finger to save me."

"Why not?" asked Oglipsi. "They have intervened everywhere else."

"Faligor is *my* experiment. When I was given charge of its development, I told the Republic I wanted no interference—so now they won't interfere even if I ask for help. This is their way of teaching a lesson to anyone who might emulate me." He paused. "Besides, Faligor has no ties to the Republic; legally they can't interfere in its internal affairs."

"But even if they cannot threaten military action,

they can institute economic reprisals," suggested Oglipsi.

"Only if they know what's going on," said Cartright.

"How can they not know?"

"Who's going to tell them? I don't know of anyone, Man or jason, who's gotten an exit visa in the past two months. And it doesn't take much to jam subspace transmissions."

"Surely some word of what has transpired here must have reached the Republic," said Oglipsi.

"Oh, probably there have been scattered reports, a few letters—though I wouldn't bet on that—and maybe even a radio transmission or two. But I don't think you have any idea just how *big* the Republic is, or how many departments there are. It's almost impossible for them to put together enough data unless it's all been sent to one agency, and I'm sure it hasn't."

"Don't the agencies speak to one another?"

Cartright smiled. "The only thing worse than no one speaking is the sound of seventeen billion voices speaking at the same time, each with its own agenda."

"I don't understand," said Oglipsi.

"Although we claim Earth as our capital, for all practical purposes Deluros VIII is the capital planet of the race of Man. Now, not only is it half a galaxy away from Faligor, but it employs eleven billion bureaucrats, each charged with keeping some infinitesimal portion of the galaxy working. Not only that, but Deluros VI was broken up into some twenty-six terraformed planetoids, each housing a government agency: the Department of Alien Affairs completely covers one planetoid; the Bureau of Taxation covers another, and so on; the military has four of the planetoids and is already cramped for space. Add to this the fact that some of the departments, like Cartography, are tens of thousands of light years away, and it becomes increasingly difficult for the right information to get into the right hands in time to do any good."

"So we can expect no help from the Republic."

"Not until we can let the right members know what's going on here," replied Cartright. "And even then, their response would be limited by the fact that Faligor is neither a Protectorate nor a member world." He sighed. "There's simply not a lot they can do, short of landing an army, and they're not going to do that."

"Do you think Labu has figured that out?" asked Oglipsi, wincing in pain as he gingerly shifted his position again.

"I doubt it. He's never struck me as being exceptionally intelligent."

"Let us hope you are right," said Oglipsi. "If he can do what he has done while acknowledging the possibility of reprisal, I fear to even think of what he might do once he knows there are no restrictions whatsoever on him."

"Amen," said Cartright softly.

Ten

It was during their third week of incarceration that Cartright and Oglipsi noticed a sudden increase of activity outside their window.

"What the devil is going on?" muttered Cartright, staring down as a team of jason laborers began uprooting the gardens in front of a governmental building.

"I do not know," replied Oglipsi, peeking out the window when Cartright stepped away. "Surely he is not planning on burying his victims right in the city center!"

"It beats me," said Cartright.

By late afternoon they had determined that a statue was being moved to the location.

"Doubtless of himself," said Cartright.

"Are you surprised?" asked Oglipsi.

"No, I suppose not," replied the human. "But it does seem a bit egomaniacal."

"His ego is the least of our worries."

The statue was delivered during the night, completely covered with tarps. For three days it remained so, some twenty feet high, an object of curiosity to all passersby. During the third day a grandstand was hastily erected in the street opposite the statue and all traffic was diverted along other routes.

"It looks," said Cartright, as the sun rose the next morning, "as if we're going to be treated to a speech by Labu himself."

"Why should you think so?" asked Oglipsi, without bothering to get to his feet and approach the window.

"Because a couple of hundred soldiers with weapons just showed up. I don't know anyone else who needs that kind of security, do you?"

The soldiers quickly secured the area, rousting moles from their shops and sending them home, searching any pedestrians in the area. Finally a holovision team from the only operating station showed up and positioned their camera and sound equipment, and then a pair of buses arrived, disgorging their passengers in front of the grandstand.

"Nothing but Men," observed Cartright. "Not a jason or a mole in the bunch." He paused. "You don't think he's going to make them all swear fealty to him, do you?"

"What has that got to do with a statue?" asked Oglipsi.

Cartright shrugged. "I suppose we'll find out in good time," he replied.

He continued watching. Most of the human were obviously there against their wills, and were forced, at gunpoint, to take seats in the grandstand. They sat in the heat and humidity for the better part of an hour, until the sound of a siren could be heard in the distance. It got louder as it approached, and at last an armored vehicle pulled up and Gama Labu, now dressed in his general's uniform, got out and walked over to the statue.

"Look at him," muttered Cartright. "He must have three hundred goddamned medals on his uniform. I'll bet my pension he can't even count that high."

Labu looked at the holo crew, who nodded, and then he climbed a small dais that had been built that morning and faced the grandstand. The Men stared at him in sullen silence until one of the soldiers said something that Cartright couldn't hear, and then a ripple of unenthusiastic applause spread through them.

"Ladies and gentlemen, thank you very much," said Labu in Terran.

"I see he's learned three new words," said Cartright caustically.

"Thank you, thank you," repeated Labu, finally raising his hands to signal an end to the applause.

"I know," he continued in the Maringo dialect, "what some of you think of me." Again he held up a hand, against an anticipated protest. "No, no, it is all right. This is Faligor, where you are free to think as you please. We do not need a constitution to guarantee you *that* right."

He paused and smiled a very alien smile, his golden fur rippling in the hot breeze that whipped across the city center.

"Many of you think that Gama Labu has no love for your race, that he does not hear your protests, that he wants to rid his planet of you. I assure you, my good friends, that this is not true. There is much about the race of Man to admire. You are not like the moles, who seek only to get rich off the sweat of other races. You have a glorious history, with many great heroes and heroines in it. You have conquered half a galaxy, and while you have not conquered Faligor, that does not make your achievement any the less admirable."

"What the hell is he getting at?" said Cartright.

"I know that some of you think me ignorant, because I do not speak or read Terran, but I am not ignorant. I know your history well. My close associate, Colonel George Witherspoon, has told me your history, and has translated many of your books for me."

"Aloud, no doubt," muttered Cartright.

"There is no reason why we should not be friends. I know that many of your people have left Faligor, but that is because they did not make an attempt to understand me or my people. In my greatness, in my open-mindedness, I do not choose only jasons for my heroes. In fact, I spit on the memories of Disanko and Robert Tantram. I have chosen for my hero a member not of my race but of your own, and I have ordered a statue of him to stand guard over the city of Romulus. Surely this will cement the ties between

Man and jason, and prove to you that I harbor no ill will toward your people.''

A small band emerged from the government building and played a discordant jason march on their various instruments, while Labu stood at attention. When they were through, he fumbled around the tarp for a moment, finally found the rope he was looking for, and gave it a sharp yank. The tarp came away to reveal a huge statue of an unimpressive-looking man dressed in a fashion that was almost a millennium out of date. The audience sat still, as if stunned.

"Who is it?'' asked Oglipsi, who had walked over to the window. "Some hero from your ancient past?''

Cartright shook his head. "I wish it was. That is a statue of Conrad Bland.''

"I am not familiar with the name. Who was Conrad Bland?''

"In the history of my race, we have had our share of genocidal maniacs: Caligula, Adolph Hitler, Joseph Stalin. The worst of them by far, the greatest killer of them all, was Conrad Bland. Before he was finally hunted down on the planet of Walpurgis III, he was responsible for the deaths of more than thirty million human beings.'' Cartright paused. "And that is Gama Labu's hero.''

Down on the street, Labu was waiting for the applause that was not forthcoming. Finally he stepped forward again.

"Conrad Bland, like myself, was a visionary, capable of great things. The only difference between us is that he was hounded to his death, while in this enlightened age I have become the president of my planet." Labu grinned again. "I realize that you are moved to silence by this act of brotherhood, but this should be a joyous occasion. The spirit of Conrad Bland lives again."

He nodded to the leader of his soldiers, who barked a command, and this time all but three men and a woman got to their feet and cheered unenthusiastically. The four who remained seated were immediately taken away by the soldiers, and Cartright lost sight of them.

Shortly thereafter, Labu's vehicle carried him away, the soldiers moved the humans back onto their buses, and things slowly went back to normal. The moles began returning to their shops, a few Men went about their business, jasons crowded around the statue and read the inscription at its base.

"He's insane!" said Cartright, sitting back down on the floor. "He's absolutely certifiable."

"No, my friend," answered Oglipsi. "He is not insane, and if you hope to oppose him, you must understand that."

"You think his actions are those of a rational being?" demanded Cartright.

"His actions are those of a barbarian, which indeed he is," answered Oglipsi, "but not a mad barbarian, which he is not. He calculates every move very carefully. Never forget that, friend Arthur."

"Just what kind of calculation goes into erecting a statue of Conrad Bland?" asked Cartright.

"It is obvious that Labu wants all Men to leave the

planet. Most of them have already left Faligor, but a few thousand diehards like yourself remain. If he starts slaughtering you, he is afraid that the Republic will come here in force—and while they may not help the jasons, or re-appropriate the human property that was stolen, there is every likelihood that a widespread massacre of humans will indeed bring the Navy here." Oglipsi paused. "So what does he do? He unveils a statue of the greatest killer in history and claims that it is his hero. There are twelve thousand humans currently on Faligor. How many do you think will be here next week?"

"I see your point," said Cartright.

"I do not think you see it in its entirety," said Oglipsi.

"What do you mean?"

"I told you: he has a reason for everything he does."

"I know. And the reason he put up the statue was to encourage humans to leave the planet."

"You are missing the point."

"I am?"

"This is a barbarian, brought up to hate not just the Enkoti, but *all* tribes that are not his own. Why do you think he wants all Men to leave the planet?"

Cartright simply stared at Oglipsi.

"Yes," said the jason. "The worst is yet to come."

Eleven

Cartright was dreaming that he was a child again, going fishing with his father on a clear blue lake, when he became aware of an insistent prodding. He moaned, tried to roll over, and pulled his blanket over himself, but the prodding became harder, and suddenly he sat up.

"You!" said a uniformed jason who had been poking him with the barrel of a sonic rifle. "Up!"

The jason turned to Oglipsi, who was huddled in a corner of the cell. "You too!"

The two of them, terrified, got to their feet, and were half-marched, half-dragged down a corridor to a staircase. They descended to ground level, and were taken to a small room where Cartright was sure they were to be tortured and killed. Instead, they were met by an overweight jason in a colonel's uniform who sat behind a scarred, battered desk.

"Arthur Cartright, Reverend James Oglipsi, all

charges against you have been dropped and you are free to leave," announced the colonel.

For just an instant Cartright thought that Labu had been overthrown, but a glance through the window assured him that the military was still going about its business.

"I thank you," Oglipsi said.

"Do not thank me. If I had my way, you would have been executed the day you arrived. You owe your gratitude to the ruler you have so unfairly slandered."

"President Labu?" said Cartright.

"President-For-Life Labu," the jason corrected him. "In honor of his new position, which was conferred upon him last night, he has ordered that one in every five political prisoners be granted their freedom. Your names were drawn." The jason glared at them. "Now get out of here. I do not wish to be in the company of either of you."

Cartright felt an urge to race out the door before the jason could change his mind, and found that the only reason he walked slowly toward his freedom was that his incarceration had left him too weak to move any faster. He and Oglipsi made their way to the street, where they turned and faced each other.

"Will you be remaining on Faligor?" asked Oglipsi.

"It is my home," answered Cartright. "And I won't let Gama Labu or anyone else drive me away." He paused. "And you—what are your plans?"

"I have my church and my flock," said Oglipsi. "I must return to them."

"Be careful what you say," said Cartright. "I can't imagine that he's not having us watched."

"I will do what I must do," said Oglipsi. He extended his golden hand. "God go with you, Arthur."

"And with you," said Cartright.

Oglipsi turned and started walking away, and Cartright found that he had to lean against the side of a building to steady himself. *Well,* he thought wryly, *I'd been wanting to lose thirty pounds for some time now. I suppose instead of being bitter I should thank them.*

A wave of dizziness overcame him, and he waited until it passed, then walked away from the jail as rapidly as he could. He turned into a side street and approached a restaurant, then saw the proprietor lock the front door when he got within a few feet of it.

I can't say that I blame you, thought Cartright. *I've been three weeks without a shave or a bath or a change of clothes; I must look like Death warmed over.* Belatedly it occurred to him that even had the restaurant allowed him inside, he had no money to pay for his food; he had been so anxious to leave the jail he hadn't asked for the return of his personal effects, nor had he any intention of going back to ask for them. Besides, the odds were that some jason had appropriated them within five minutes of his incarceration.

He didn't even possess a coin for a newspaper, but he pulled a used one out of a garbage can and quickly skimmed it. The lead story, of course, was Labu's appointment—self-appointment, really—as President-For-Life. In honor of the event, the government had renamed the Jonathan Ramsey National Park as the Gama Labu National Park. The Bortai River was now the Labu River, and the Bularoki Reserve, one of the prime attractions for tourists, was now the Batisha Reserve, named in honor of Labu's youngest wife.

He was wondering if he possessed the strength to undertake the three-mile walk to his home, which was just beyond the city limits, when a vehicle pulled up and Dorothy Watts, a neighbor, offered him a ride.

"Thank you," he said, getting into the vehicle.

"We thought we'd lost you," she said as he closed the door. "People have this habit of simply vanishing these days."

"He won't kill any Men," said Cartright. "He may be crazy, but he's not stupid."

"Well, truth to tell, there aren't that many of us left," said Watts. "I think half of us have left the planet in the past two weeks."

"I'm glad to see you stayed."

"Oh, I'm leaving, too. I have tickets on the flight to Pollux IV three days from now." She paused. "I assume you'll be leaving soon yourself?"

Cartright shook his head. "Somebody's got to stay and put things right."

"Arthur, it was a noble experiment, and maybe if Bobby had won the election, things would have turned out all right. But you can't deal with Labu and you can't reason with him. It's just a matter of time before he forces all the moles and Men to leave. At least if I go now, I can get some mole to buy my farm. If I wait until I'm kicked off the planet, Labu will wind up owning it, and I'll kill the stock and poison the wells before I let that happen."

"I'm sorry you feel that way," said Cartright.

"I'm sorry you don't. At least I'll be alive at this time next year."

"So will I. If he didn't kill me this time, he won't ever kill me."

She shrugged. "I hope you're right."

"Things will get better," insisted Cartright.

"What makes you think so?"

"If for no other reason, the fact that you and the rest of the humans who leave will report what's been going on."

"So what?" she said. "Do you think the Republic is going to send the Navy here to stop a jason from killing other jasons and robbing the moles? They'll just shake their heads sadly, say that it's simply another example of what happens when you civilize primitive races too quickly and then leave them to their own devices, and twenty years from now some bleeding heart foundation on Deluros VIII might start a fund for those jasons who have suffered the most. And if they do, the fund will go right into the private bank account of Labu or whoever's in charge."

"He's only been in power for a year. We can undo the damage in even less time."

"Without overthrowing him?" she demanded. "Are *you* going to lead the charge against the presidential palace?"

"Someone will," said Cartright. "Some jason."

"What will he storm the barricades with? Sticks and stones?"

"I don't know," admitted Cartright. "But I'm not prepared to cut and run, just because I don't know. There must be a way."

She took her eyes off the road and stared at him, not without sympathy. "Arthur, I know how much this planet means to you, how much of yourself you've put into it, and I'm sorry things have turned out this way—but has it ever occurred to you that the situation will get a lot worse before it gets any better?"

"These are decent beings," said Cartright adamantly. "They won't put up with this forever."

"Probably not," she agreed. "But I'm fifty-three years old. I haven't *got* forever—and neither have you." She paused. "Look at them, Arthur. They play at government. They sit around and make motions and have no idea what they're doing. When they want money, they print it up, and when it turns out to be no good, they confiscate whatever they want from the moles' stores. They kill all the animals in the national parks for target practice, and then they can't understand why the tourist industry has died. They close down churches and erect statues to Conrad Bland. They're *savages,* Arthur. You did your best, but you've tried to move them too far too fast. Nobody blames you for it, but it's time you realized what you're dealing with here. Why should they obey the laws of civilized worlds? Nobody had even heard of those laws a generation ago. They tried to be a democracy and they wound up with William Barioke. They tried to correct that mistake and they got Gama Labu." She stared at him. "Do you really have much confidence in whoever they replace Labu with?"

"There must be a way."

She stared at him again, sighed wearily, and drove the rest of the way to his house in silence.

When Cartright unlocked the door and went inside, he was not surprised to find that it had been thoroughly looted, and that his servants—all Enkoti—weren't on the premises. Most of the furniture was gone, except for his kitchen set and one easy chair, his computers were missing, his holovisions had been stolen, and his pantry was empty. All insurance on Faligor had been cancelled within a month of Labu's coup, but he methodically made a list of what was missing and ordered replacements from the few dependable local stores. He found a few containers of soup that the looters had overlooked or simply hadn't wanted, warmed a bowl and decided that it was about all his system could handle at present anyway, and then took the first shower he'd had in a month and collapsed on his bed. He slept for nineteen hours, awoke, and drove out to buy some supplies and a small holovision set. When he returned he made himself some porridge and turned on the holovision.

The announcer, dressed—as they all seemed to be dressed these days—in a military uniform, was reading a weather forecast, which didn't take much effort: the weather was the same as always, moderate, temperate, with a brief afternoon shower. When he was done, he recapped the top news stories of the previous day: Labu's exalted new title, the name changes, the fact that amnesty had been declared for all prisoners (there was no mention of the one-in-five provision, or that it was for political prisoners only), and then there was a final item concerning the Reverend James Oglipsi, who had just returned from a three-week vacation to the Gama Labu (formerly Jonathan Ramsey) National Park.

Evidently Oglipsi, a good friend of President Labu, had been attacked by crazed religious fanatics on his way home. For reasons unknown, they had tortured and finally crucified him. (A holograph of Oglipsi's terribly mutilated body was flashed on the screen, still on its cross.) The perpetrators had been apprehended and incarcerated, but the army regretfully arrived on the scene too late to save the beloved religious leader.

President-For-Life Labu was shocked by the death of his friend, and had announced that if Christianity could make otherwise reasonable being commit so perverse a crime, then from this day forth Christianity would be banned on Faligor. Oglipsi himself would receive a hero's funeral tomorrow afternoon; the President-For-Life regretted that affairs of state prevented him from attending, but he would send one of his wives, not Batisha but one of the older ones, in his place as his personal representative.

Cartright stared numbly at the holograph of the jason he had seen just the previous day, and the image remained in his mind long after he had shut off the holovision. The dead eyes seemed to be staring directly into his soul, saying, *I told you so, Arthur. He is not a madman, but a clever barbarian, and once more he has gotten what he wants.*

I will pray for your soul, my friend, answered Cartright silently.

Why? Oglipsi's image seemed to ask. *It is you who are in Hell, not I.*

Twelve

Gama Labu knew better that to leave Faligor and pay state visits throughout the galaxy. After all, that was how he usurped power from William Barioke. But there were things out there that he wanted, and he set about trying to obtain them.

Canphor VI and VII, known as the Canphor Twins, had developed all kinds of weaponry over the centuries in their continual wars with Mankind's Republic. Most of the weapons were obsolete, but only because the Republic had learned how to counter or negate them. They would still function on Faligor, where the most powerful weapon that could be mounted against the government was a laser rifle, and so Labu played host to a delegation of Canphorites, both the tall blue beings from Canphor VI and the short, burly, tripodal, red-hued beings from Canphor VII. They dined sumptuously, were entertained lavishly, and in the end they consented to supply

Faligor with a few hundred weapons in exchange for the next year's production of silver and platinum from the mines. They never asked if the mines were still fully operational, and Labu never told them that eighty percent of them had been shut down due to his inability to pay for labor or replacement parts. By the time they found out, it was too late to reclaim the weapons, all of which had been strategically dispersed and most of which were already in various stages of disrepair.

Labu then confounded the remaining Men on Faligor by publicly converting to Judaism, and offering the world of New Jerusalem an embassy in Remus. He unconverted just as quickly when it became apparent that no Men of any faith were going to supply him with weapons simply because he professed to share their religion.

His conversions and unconversions became a public joke, until he hit upon an arcane idol-worshipping faith practiced by the Domarians, a stilt-legged race that spent most of their lives following their sun as it receded over their horizon. The Domarians supplied him with weapons and hard currency, and Rainche, their religion, soon became the official state religion of Faligor. It was just as well that the Domarians were chlorine breathers who were physically unable to visit Faligor, or they might have noticed that not a single religious edifice or idol had been constructed.

While Labu had been amassing his weaponry, Romulus and Remus had been spared any serious disruptions. True, two or three jasons turned up missing every day, and some moles vanished while on a picnic, and a number of local businesses were looted and burned, but no weapons of mass destruction had been turned on the populace, there were no massacres such as had occurred in the past, the cities continued to limp along. When Labu put his soldiers to work repairing the highway between the two cities, a handful of the remaining Men came to the conclusion that now that he had his military toys and was the unquestioned leader of Faligor that he might actually have decided to try to do something constructive, if not to assure an honored place in the history books, then simply because there was no more power to be grabbed and he might as well put that which he had accumulated to use.

That conclusion lasted until the morning that his troops surrounded the Republic's embassy in Romulus, trained their most powerful weaponry on the building, and demanded that the ambassador and his staff of seventeen present themselves for arrest on a charge of subversion. For proof, Labu went on holovision and furiously waved a captured message from the ambassador to Deluros VIII, calling him a tyrant and suggesting that he was responsible for the genocide of a minor tribe in the far north, where his soldiers had secretly been testing their weaponry.

The Republic responded by demanding the release of all embassy personnel. Labu refused.

And three days later the sky of Faligor was black with ships, some six hundred in all, as the Navy delivered an ultimatum: release our people within twenty-four hours or suffer the consequences.

Labu made no reply for fifteen hours, then went on holovision again to point out that he had never intended to *keep* the ambassador and his staff incarcerated, but simply refused to let them return to the embassy. He had no desire, he continued, to go to war with the Republic, which had completely misinterpreted his motives, and if the Commander of the 43rd Fleet would agree to take the undesirables off the planet, he would release them forthwith.

The Navy did not answer, and four hours later, screaming his imprecations before the cameras, he ordered the immediate release and deportation of his prisoners, proclaiming to his people that only his willingness to humiliate himself before the warmongering Republic had saved the planet from total devastation. The ambassadorial personnel were released two hours before the deadline, rushed to the spaceport at Remus, and flow up to the flagship. The next morning the skies were empty again, and Labu looked about for some way to re-establish his authority.

He didn't have to look far.

It was obvious to him that he could not confront the Republic. It was just as obvious that most of his people were aware of that fact. He had shown weakness, and that had to be countered with a show of strength. He needed an enemy, a race—unlike Man—that he could dominate, and he just happened to have one on his planet: the moles.

What were they doing here in the first place? he demanded. Why were they taking jobs and running businesses that by rights should have been owned by jasons?

You think, he pointed out, that they have been trying to assimilate themselves into our society by learning our language and respecting our customs, but you are wrong. Their sole purpose is to subvert and control our economy. They have infiltrated every level of our society except the government, hoping that if they were quiet enough we wouldn't notice what they were doing. But *I* have noticed, said Labu, and I have seen enough.

The government's propaganda machine, which heretofore had existed only to praise Labu, soon began attacking the moles. Were their children in the schools? They were taking up space that should have been occupied by jason children. Throw them out. Were their houses bigger and grander than the jasons'? They built them with jason money. Throw them out. Did they practice their own religious rituals, read their own books, keep to themselves? They were mocking the jasons, trying to show that they were superior to them. Throw them out.

Colonel Witherspoon waited until the propaganda began working, then turned his soldiers loose in the major cities across the planet. Moles began disappearing with the same regularity as jasons. Government buildings, most of them standing empty and useless, were put to the torch, and moles were arrested and executed for the fires.

Finally Labu took to the air once more to announce what he called his Mole Policy: all moles had sixty days to leave the planet. They could take nothing with them—not possessions, not food, not money. Any mole remaining on Faligor past the appointed day would be in breach of the law and summarily executed for high treason.

The moles protested as vigorously as they could. Many of them had been born on Faligor. They had lived there, worked there, paid their taxes there, put up with discrimination, and now they were being thrown out with nothing more than the clothing on their backs. Even if they wanted to obey the law, there weren't enough commuter ships to begin to accommodate them, and since Faligor's currency was worthless anywhere else in the galaxy, they could not charter ships from other worlds.

Finally some of the alien embassies, seeing a chance to win the moles' home world to their cause, arranged for a contingent of rescue ships to come to Faligor and begin taking the moles off the planet. Labu decided to make their lot easier by systematically rounding up the moles from all over the planet and transporting them to detention camps until they could be taken offworld.

It was a remarkable operation for a relatively undeveloped world. In less than sixty days some seven million moles were transported to the detention camps; all but four hundred thousand were taken off the planet, and Labu allowed the ships an extra week to rescue the remainder.

When the last of the moles had gone—the few who steadfastly refused to leave were being systematically hunted down by Witherspoon's troops—Labu addressed his people again.

Faligor, he informed them, is pure for the first time in a generation. With all our external enemies gone, like the moles, or held at bay, like the Republic, it is almost time to start building our Utopia.

Just as soon, he added, as we eliminate the enemies within.

Thirteen

Cartright was preparing his morning coffee when there was a knock at the front door. His first inclination was to hide, but he knew it would be useless. If they had come for him, they'd find him.

His second inclination was to get his gun, but there was always a chance they just wanted him for questioning, or to inform on a neighbor, and the sight of a gun in his hand might result in an instant retaliation from one of Labu's thugs.

So he finally settled for sighing deeply, taking a deep breath, and walking to the front door. There was no sense commanding it to open, since there was no power, as was the case more and more often these days, so instead he reached out, grabbed the handle, and turned it—and found himself facing Susan Beddoes.

"Arthur, are you all right?" she asked, quickly stepping inside and steadying him. "You look like you're about to collapse."

"A nervous reaction," he said, quickly shutting the door behind her. "What in the world are you doing here, Susan?"

"Didn't you get my message? I sent it via subspace radio two days ago."

"I haven't gotten any subspace messages in more than three months."

"I sent one."

"I believe you," replied Cartright, leading her into his shabby living room. "Please, come in and sit down. How are you?"

"I'm well, thank you. That's more than I can say for Faligor."

"Why have you come back?"

"Ezra and Martha Simpson died. I'm here for their funeral."

"That was stupid, Susan, just plain stupid. They died four weeks ago."

"I just got word of it two days ago. I sent a message asking when the funeral would be held, and they responded that it would be tomorrow."

"Whoever you contacted doesn't even know who the Simpsons were," said Cartright wearily.

"But why would they say—?"

"You had to pay two hundred credits for your visa, and there's a one hundred-credit exit fee," said Cartright. "Faligor is desperate for hard currency. You're worth three hundred credits to them. More, in fact, since no other world is allowed to land commercial spaceliners here, so you unquestionably paid one of the government-owned ships at least another thousand credits to get you to Faligor." He paused. "Where are you staying?"

"I have a room at the Imperial Remus Hotel," answered Beddoes.

"For which they will not accept payment in local currency unless you're a jason," said Cartright. "As long as you're here, you'll stay with me. At least that's *some* money that Labu won't get his hands on."

Beddoes was silent for a moment. "How bad is it here, really?" she asked at last.

"I don't know how it can get much worse," replied Cartright. "You heard about the moles?"

She nodded. "How could he get away with that?"

"At least they're alive," said Cartright, ignoring her question. "He's been methodically decimating the minor tribes for the past year. There's no way to know the actual body count, and of course the government denies any responsibility, but I'd be surprised if he hasn't killed off at least a million jasons."

"A million?" said Beddoes unbelievingly.

"At least."

"I knew he was insane, but I had no idea . . ."

"For the longest time I believed what a jason friend told me, that he wasn't crazy at all, that he was just a barbarian exercising maniacal power on behalf of his tribe," said Cartright. "But now . . . I just don't know." He paused. "I do know that whether he's insane or not, he's committing genocide on a scale that hasn't been seen since the heyday of Conrad Bland."

"How about *you*, Arthur?" asked Beddoes seriously. "Are you safe?"

"Nobody's really safe, but at least he's still leaving most of the Men alone."

"What about the Simpsons?"

Cartright shrugged. "I don't know."

"How did they die?"

"Their house was broken into, and they were bludgeoned to death by the looters."

"Then he *is* responsible."

"Possibly, possibly not," said Cartright. "He's got half a million soldiers who loot so many places and kill so many beings that it's possible they murdered the Simpsons on their own. After all, it's what they've been trained to do."

"Isn't there any way to find out?"

Cartright shook his head. "We don't have a police state here, Susan. We have a state of terror. You don't ask questions in a police state; you don't even *think* about them in a state of terror." He stared at her for a long moment. "When's the next flight out of here?"

"Three days," she replied. "Faligor's not getting a lot of traffic these days."

"I want you on it. You can stay here until then."

She nodded. "You get no arguments from me."

They sat in silence for a few moments.

"It used to be so beautiful here," she said at last, looking out a window toward the Hills of Heaven, which were shrouded in mist.

"It could be again."

"Not in your lifetime, Arthur."

"My lifetime is measured from one day to the next," he said with a wry smile. "The planet will go on. Gama Labu can't live forever; from what I've seen, he's eating himself into an early grave."

"Not early enough," answered Beddoes. "Why do you stay?"

"It's my creation," he said. "If I don't stay, who will?"

"No one," she replied, "and Faligor will be all the better for it."

He shook his head. "We can't put it back the way it was, Susan. For better or worse, they have cities and roads and schools and a written language—"

"And guns," she added.

"And guns," he acknowledged. "If I could leave and they could all somehow magically go back to living as they did in Disanko's day, I'd be out of here on the next spaceflight. But they can't. Pandora's box is wide open."

"But what purpose do you serve by staying?"

"No purpose at all," he said. "But I'm the architect of their disaster, and even if I can't fix it, I can't turn my back on it and simply walk away. God may have flooded the Earth, but He never turned His back on it."

"Need I point out that you're not God?" said Beddoes.

"I know I'm not God. I'm not even a mildly competent human being. That's all the more reason why I can't turn my back on Faligor."

"I don't understand your reasoning at all, Arthur. We did our best. You can't blame yourself because

some madman like Gama Labu comes out of nowhere and takes over the world.''

"If it wasn't for us, he'd be the headman in a
village of maybe four hundred at most. How much
damage could he have done there?''

"Arthur, you're blaming yourself for everything,''
she said. "The jasons have to take some responsibility for their own actions.''

He shrugged. "I can't help the way I feel, any
more than you could help the repugnance you felt
the first time you saw Labu. Do you remember that
day?''

"I remember it.''

He smiled wanly. "I should have listened to you.''

"Would it have done any good?''

He considered her question. "Probably not.''

"Well, then?''

"That doesn't change anything, Susan. I'm staying.''

"All right, you're staying.'' She paused. "I notice
that the power's off.''

"It comes and goes.''

"And the water?''

"If I don't boil it for coffee, I purify it.''

"Does *anything* work anymore?''

"The weapons, of course—though I'm told he
can't get spare parts for them. And the roads, so he
can move his army quickly from one spot to another.
Not much else. Mail service is sporadic at best, and
the phones haven't worked in months.''

"That's what happens when you start by killing
off the intellectuals and the technicians.''

"How did you know he'd done that?"

"Eventually it's what all dictators do. Usually they build the roads first, though. The one I was on looks like it was recently resurfaced."

Suddenly Cartright was aware of a blinking off to his right. He turned and saw that his clock was functioning again.

"The power's back on," he announced, getting to his feet. "Let me reset the security system, and then I'll fix us some coffee."

"How long was it out?" asked Beddoes.

"Only five or six hours this time. They're getting better about it."

She walked over to the holovision. "Do you get any entertainment on this?"

He shook his head. "A couple of hours a day of government speeches, a few heavily-censored news reports, and twenty hours of day of Praise God commercials."

"Praise God commercials?" she repeated curiously.

"Every business in Romulus and Remus buys a minute or two of time to praise the Lord for blessing our world by giving us Gama Labu as our president. The ones that don't take out the ads usually aren't around a month later." He paused and shrugged. "You might as well turn it on. Who knows? Maybe we can catch a newscast."

She activated the holovision while he finished preparing the coffee, and was treated to some fifteen or twenty Praise God commercials. Then suddenly the screen went blank.

"Power failure again?" she asked.

Cartright shook his head. "No, the coffee's still brewing. Maybe the problem's at the studio's end."

The screen remained blank while Cartright poured the coffee, and then he and Susan sat down at the kitchen table, discussing old friends and old times. They had totally forgotten the holovision when suddenly it came to life. A slender jason, his expression somber, held a sheet of paper in his hand.

"I have an emergency announcement," he said in urgent tones. "Last night a spaceliner registered to the Republic world of Barios IV and carrying some three hundred pasengers, most of them members of the race of Man, was hijacked by a group of fourteen Lodinites."

"Why does that make the news *here?*" asked Beddoes.

"The ship landed at the Remus spaceport thirty minutes ago. The Lodinites, through the good offices of President-For-Life Labu, have contacted the Republic and offered to exchange their hostages for the release of some forty-two hundred Lodinites currently being incarcerated on various worlds of the Republic. There has been no response as yet."

"Here it comes," muttered Cartright.

The announcer paused for a moment and peered into the camera.

"Until this situation has been resolved, the spaceport has been closed and all transients will have to remain on Faligor."

Fourteen

During the first few hours of the crisis, Cartright and Beddoes sat in front of the holo set, waiting impatiently for details that were not forthcoming. Finally, in early evening, another announcer reported that there was still no answer from the Republic, and that a man and two women had been shot attempting to escape from their captors. The man had died, and the two women were back with the rest of the hostages, their condition unknown. President-For-Life Labu intended to maintain strict neutrality, and therefore would not offer any medical assistance, but if any Men on the planet wished to help the hostages . . .

"Arthur, have you got a medical kit here at the house?" asked Beddoes when the bulletin was finished.

"Surely you're not thinking of going to the spaceport?" demanded Cartright. "We have human doctors here. *They'll* take care of the hostages."

"It's an excuse to get in there," replied Beddoes.

"Why do you *want* to get in there?"

"Sooner or later the hostages are going to be released or rescued," said Beddoes. "Probably sooner. I think there's every chance they'll get off the planet before I do, and I want some of them to know what's been going on here and carry the story back, just in case I'm stuck here. Showing up with a med kit will at least give me access to them."

"But you're totally untrained!" protested Cartright. "They'll never let you through."

"I have a doctorate in entomology," she replied. "It's on my passport and all my identification cards. And just between you and me, I don't think the guards around the spaceport will know one type of doctor from another." She paused. "Have you got one?"

"An identification card?" he asked, confused.

"A medical kit."

"Yes," replied Cartright. "I suppose as long as you're going there, I might as well drive you there myself."

"Thank you, Arthur. I appreciate it." She paused. "I don't think it would be a wise idea for you to try to enter the spaceport, though. They know who you are, and they'll know you don't have any medical experience."

"You might need me," he said. "Most of Labu's soldiers don't speak Terran."

"It's all right," she assured him. "I used to live here, remember? My Maringo is a little rusty, but I can make myself understood."

Cartright went upstairs and came back down a few minutes later, carrying a lightweight medical kit.

"How long do you think you'll be there?"

She shrugged. "I have no idea. If the hostages' wounds are superficial, possibly no more than an hour. If it's serious, or if some misguided local Men make an ill-considered protest, it could be a few days." She smiled. "Which is a roundabout way of saying: don't wait for me. If they're ransomed or rescued and I see a way to leave with them, I won't be back at all."

"They won't be ransomed," said Cartright. "That would just encourage half a hundred other races to start taking hostages. You could be in for a long stay."

"I won't be any worse off there than stuck out here, waiting for the situation to be resolved so I can go to the spaceport. At least I'll be right there if some opportunity to leave should present itself."

Cartright walked to the door. "All right," he said. "I suppose we might as well be on our way."

They came to the first roadblock a mile out of the city. Beddoes displayed her medical kit and explained that she was answering President-For-Life Labu's request for help, and they were waved through. The process was repeated at five more road blocks, and at last they reached the gate of the spaceport, where the interrogation was more aggressive and extended, but finally one of the guards told Beddoes to get out of the vehicle. He frisked her, then told her to follow him, and began leading her toward the main lobby of the spaceport while Cartright waved to her and turned his vehicle toward home.

She was escorted through the entrance, then down a broad corridor past rows of jason soldiers to a large waiting room. Here, after an extended conversation between two jasons and a trio of heavily armed Lodinites, she was turned over to the latter, who took her into the room.

Three hundred men and women and a handful of other races were standing and sitting around the room, most of them looking terrified and shell-shocked, and two women lay on the floor while a young male doctor worked on their wounds.

"Thank goodness you've come!" said the doctor, looking briefly at Beddoes. "I don't think this one"—he indicated one of the women—"is going to make it. Massive internal hemorrhaging, and she's lost an awful lot of blood. Do what you can for her, while I keep working on the other one."

Beddoes walked over and knelt down next to him. "I'm not a doctor or a nurse," she said in low tones. "Just tell me what to do."

He turned to her, his eyes wide. "You're part of a rescue team?" he whispered.

She shook her head. "No."

"Then what are you—"

"Keep your voice down," said Beddoes, "and just tell me what to do."

"There's nothing we *can* do under these circumstances," replied the doctor. "Just do your best to make the patient comfortable, and if you know how to take a pulse, give me a reading every four or five minutes.''

Beddoes nodded and did as she was instructed. After a few moments, she gestured to a bystander, a middle-aged man who was watching her intently, his tunic soaked with sweat.

''Are you related to this woman?'' asked Beddoes.

''No.''

''All right. The Lodinites won't know it for a while yet, but she's dead. *Don't react!*'' she whispered harshly. ''It's essential that I remain here. I want you to circulate among the hostages, and see to it that someone faints, or comes down with stomach cramps, or in some other way demonstrates a need for medical attention, every hour or so. Do you understand?''

''Yes,'' whispered the man excitedly. ''Are we being rescued?''

''I have no idea,'' said Beddoes. ''I just know that I need to remain here. Will you help me?''

''Yes,'' repeated the man. He soon began walking among the hostages, stopping to speak to those he knew.

A moment later the doctor looked at Beddoes' patient, sighed, and placed a towel over her face.

''Damn it!'' snapped Beddoes. ''It would have been another half hour before the Lodinites knew she was dead.''

''You didn't want them to know?'' asked the doctor, confused.

''No.''

''Why not?''

"I don't want them to send me away."

"Who *are* you?" demanded the doctor.

"Just someone who wants to get off the planet—or at least get some information off it."

"You willingly put yourself in the Lodinites' hands?" he asked incredulously.

"The Lodinites are the least of your problems," replied Beddoes. "Now tell me what I can do so it will look like I'm helping you."

He instructed her on how to care for those hostages who were less seriously ill while he labored over the wounded woman. After half an hour had passed, she became aware of a sudden silence, and turned to see that Gama Labu himself, clad in his now-familiar military uniform, had entered the room.

"Good morning," said the President-For-Life, ignoring the fact that it was still the middle of the night. "I am President-For-Life Gama Labu, and I bid you welcome. Thank you very much."

Overwhelming silence greeted his statement.

"Thank you very much," he repeated. He looked quickly around the room. "Maringo?" he asked.

Beddoes stood up. "I speak Maringo," she said.

Labu stared at her curiously. "Don't I know you?" he asked in the native dialect.

"I do not believe so, Mr. President," she answered. "I am just a visitor to Faligor."

"Then how did you learn Maringo?" he asked. "And my title is not President, but President-For-Life."

"I lived on Faligor many years ago," answered Beddoes.

He continued to stare unblinking at her. "And we have never met?"

"Not formally," she said. "I was there the day you defeated Billy Wycynski."

Suddenly Labu smiled. "Ah! Then we are old friends!" He chuckled. "I was quite wonderful that day, was I not?"

"You were, Mr. President-For-Life."

He hunched over in an ungainly crouch. "Right-right-left-right," he said happily. "And that was the end of the human champion."

"It was a memorable performance," agreed Beddoes, aware that none of the hostages could understand a word that was being said, and wondering how they would interpret Labu's shadow-boxing.

"Yes, it was," agreed Labu. Suddenly he was all business again. "Stand beside me and translate for me."

Beddoes walked over to Labu's side, resisting the urge to shudder as he placed a huge, friendly hand on her shoulder.

"Greetings, my friends," said Labu, "and welcome to Faligor. I am President-For-Life Gama Labu, and you are my guests." He waited for Beddoes to translate, then continued. "Due to a most unfortunate circumstance, you have been brought to this room by force. Since we are a neutral world that desires no one's enmity, I am unhappily not able to set you free, but I am working behind the scenes to get the Republic to release its Lodinite prisoners, and

I am sure we will soon reach an accommodation. In the meantime, I will see to it that you are well-fed and that you receive whatever medical attention you require. I regret that I cannot do anything more, but it is the Republic that is indifferent to your fate, not I. You will notice that I wear no weapons; I am as much a prisoner on my own planet as you are."

Beddoes translated all but the last sentence, and after a moment Labu turned to her. "I understand Terran better than I speak it," he told her. "Now please translate the final sentence."

"They know better than to believe it," said Beddoes.

"Are you calling me a liar?" demanded Labu, drawing himself up to his full height and towering angrily above the human.

Beddoes looked at his face, contorted in fury, and felt the same fear that she had felt the first time she had seen him all those years ago at Emperor Bobby's mansion.

"No, sir, I am not." She turned back to the hostages and said, in Terran, "I am as much a prisoner on my own planet as you are."

The remark was greeted by sullen stares, interspersed with sardonic laughter.

"You are fools!" snapped Labu. "Just as your leaders are fools! You will all die here, and your bodies will be left out for the scavengers!"

Beddoes started to translate, and Labu laid a heavy hand on her shoulder and squeezed it hard.

"Be quiet," he said.

Labu stared at the hostages for a long moment,

then forced another smile to his lips. "I am doing what I can to gain your freedom. If you government is reasonable, I am sure we can resolve this unfortunate situation in a matter of days, perhaps hours."

Beddoes remained motionless until he prodded her with a pudgy finger.

"Translate!"

"I thought—"

"The Republic will be just as happy to receive 299 hostages as three hundred," he said softly. "Do not test me again."

Beddoes dutifully translated his words.

"Thank you very much," he said in Terran. Then he smiled, bowed, and left the room.

As the hostages began speaking among themselves in frightened whispers, a young man walked up to Beddoes and intercepted her as she was on her way back to rejoin the doctor.

"I need to speak to you," he said softly.

"What about?" she asked.

He glanced quickly around the room. "Not now. Wait until everyone's gotten over Labu's appearance, and the guards are a little less attentive."

She busied herself for about twenty minutes, then walked to a corner of the room, where the young man joined her a moment later.

"Have you any message for me?" he asked quietly.

"None."

"Think hard," he persisted. "My name is Anton McCreigh."

"No," she said. "Why should you think I do?"

"Because I'm security, and you are not a passenger."

"Security?"

"Not so loud, please."

"How many of you are here?"

"There are four of us. Ever since the Canphorites hijacked one of our spaceliners last year, a team of security personnel is on every commercial spaceflight."

"I don't remember hearing anything about a Canphorite hijacking," said Beddoes.

"We got our people out before they could even make any demands," said McCreigh. "Problem is, we lost sixty-three passengers in the process. Since then, we have trained anti-terrorists flying all the commercial flights. We have a number of contingency plans, each designed to get our people out with a minimum loss of life."

"How did you get into this fix in the first place?"

"They took over the ship while it was on the ground, and there were too many of them," answered McCreigh. "If we'd started shooting, we'd have lost too many passengers."

"Then what's the good of having security teams?" she asked.

"By now, a rescue operation has been mounted," said McCreigh. "Since you aren't a passenger, I thought you might be a part of it, or at least a messenger." He paused. "Our job is to protect the hostages once the shooting starts, and to get them out of here as quickly as possible once it's over."

"How will you know which contingency plan to use?" asked Beddoes.

"We'll be given a signal—*if* we can spot it. We've already targeted which Lodinites we ourselves will take out."

"Are you armed?"

He shook his head. "Had to leave the weapons aboard the ship. There was no way we were going to be able to get them past the spaceport scanners."

"There are fourteen heavily-armed Lodinites," noted Susan. "Are you telling me you plan to take them out with four unarmed Men?"

"We'll ignore those who are positioned to prevent a rescue attempt and those who are guarding the perimeter of the area. Our concern is disabling the six or seven who might be tempted to turn their weapons loose on the hostages as soon as they figure out that the Republic is trying to rescue them rather than trade for them."

"It sounds suicidal."

"It's *dangerous*," he corrected her. "*Suicidal* is a woman who refuses to translate what Labu wants us to hear."

"Touché," she replied. "How soon do you expect the rescue?"

He shrugged. "There's no way of knowing. The Republic could march in here and blow Labu and his whole army away if it wanted to, but that wouldn't save the hostages. Labu's probably got three thousand men or more guarding the spaceport right now. If they see us land and start shooting, it could result in the death of every person in the room. So our rescue team will have to figure out where to land, and how best to make their way to the spaceport, and how to avoid any conflict until *after* they've secured this room and protected the hostages.'' He grimaced. ''That's why I was hoping you were working for us. Any kind of information at all might save a few lives.''

''I'm sorry I'm not able to help you,'' said Beddoes.

''Then what the hell *are* you doing here?'' said McCreigh. ''I was watching you before: you're no nurse, you obviously aren't working for Labu, and you're not a hostage. So who and what are you?''

''I used to live on Faligor,'' she replied. ''I left before Labu took over. I came back for a friend's funeral, and there is every chance I may be stuck here—especially if your rescue succeeds. Labu will be so furious with the Republic that my guess is he'll cancel all exit visas and start killing every Man he can find.''

McCreigh smiled. ''So you're hoping to be mistaken for a hostage and rescued with the rest of us?''

Beddoes nodded. ''Something like that. At the very least, I want someone who is going back to the Republic to report what's going on here.''

''What's going on is that Labu is helping his Lodinite friends try to blackmail the Republic into releasing terrorist prisoners,'' answered McCreigh.

She shook her head. ''That's the least of it. He's already killed off more than a million members of his own race. He's got to be stopped before he wipes out every last living being on Faligor.''

"What he does to his own people isn't the Republic's business."

"Then it had better *become* our business!" snapped Beddoes. "We created the conditions that allowed him to come to power. He's our responsibility."

"Convincing *me* won't do you any good," said McCreigh. "I'm just a soldier."

"That's why I want the story to get to someone who *can* act on it," said Beddoes. "And since most of the hostages have more immediate concerns, that's why I want to leave the planet with them."

"Well, this much I can promise you," said McCreigh. "Everyone in this room is leaving one way or the other."

"One way or the other?" repeated Beddoes.

"On a ship or in a box—or maybe both."

Just then a man clutched his stomach and started moaning. Beddoes hoped that this was an act being performed to help her preserve her medical persona and she began tending to him. It turned out that the man had collapsed from nervous exhaustion, but his condition didn't seem life-threatening, and she did what she could to make him comfortable. His wife joined them, and in low whispers Beddoes spent the next fifteen minutes telling her what she wanted them to convey to someone in authority in case she herself did not live long enough to leave Faligor.

The rest of the night and most of the next day passed in much the same manner, with Beddoes doing what she could to help the handful of men and women who were either sick or pretending to be. By sunrise the condition of the wounded woman had stabilized, and the doctor had gone off to a corner to sleep. In midafternoon Labu again appeared to explain that negotiations were continuing, and to apologize for not being able to supply the hostages with food after all. He claimed once again that he could be of use in the negotiations only if he maintained a strict neutrality, which he had now decided meant refusing to lift a finger either to free them or make them more comfortable. An hour later he was back, this time with a pair of jasons operating a holographic camera. They trained it on the dead and wounded women, and on a man who had spent most of the night crying and now simply sat, catatonic, staring off into space.

"Your wonderful race has always been known for its compassion," announced Labu as Beddoes translated his words. "It is perhaps your most admirable quality. Once these holographs of your unfortunate state reach your leaders, I am sure that they will redouble their efforts to secure your release." He paused. "Unfortunately, since the crisis has caused the cancellation of all incoming and outgoing spaceflights, I have had to charge them for Faligor's lost revenues, but it is a small price for such an immensely wealthy race to pay, and I'm sure it will present no problem in the negotiations."

Then he and the camera crew were gone, leaving the hostages to contemplate their fate.

Beddoes went back to tending to the truly sick— there seemed to be more of them every hour—and finally, exhausted, she walked over to a wall, sat down, and propped her back up against it. A moment later McCreigh sat down next to her, leaned against the wall, and closed his eyes.

"Are you awake?" he whispered.

"Yes."

"It'll be tonight."

"They've signaled you already?" she asked. "How?"

"No, they haven't signaled anyone yet."

"Then how do you know?"

"It's our experience that once the kidnappers realize that we're not negotiating in good faith, that we're stalling for time, they tend to disperse the captives so that a rescue operation becomes an impossibility—so we're geared to go into action a maximum of forty-eight hours after capture. That'll be sometime tonight."

"Why are you telling me all this?" asked Beddoes.

"Because you've been staring at me all day, and as the others fall asleep and the guards spend more time watching the rest of us, I don't want them putting two and two together."

"I wasn't aware that I was looking at you," said Beddoes.

"So far I don't think the Lodinites are aware of it either," said McCreigh. "Let's keep it that way."

"What do I do when the rescue begins?"

"Nothing."

"Surely I can help in some way," she said. "Cause a distraction, perhaps, or—"

"Just hit the deck and scream a lot, like everyone else. You start running around, you'll probably get yourself shot. At the very least, you're as likely to distract the good guys as the bad guys."

She sighed. "Whatever you say."

"*That's* what I say." He paused. "Just believe me when I tell you that I'm good at my job."

He stood up, stretched, walked to a darker section of the room, and lay down.

Beddoes realized that she was becoming drowsy, that she hadn't slept in close to forty hours, and she shut her eyes. She could sleep for an hour, perhaps an hour and a half, she decided; then she'd be fresh for the danger that would follow. An hour and a half, that would do it; perhaps two . . .

She awoke with a start to the hum of laser guns and the screams of dying Lodinites. McCreigh was standing over the body of one of their captors, whose head was twisted at a grotesque angle, and she saw another man and two women making swift work of three other Lodinites. Then armed men were bursting in through the windows, Lodinites were entering with blazing weapons through a pair of doors, jasons were firing aimlessly in the semidarkness of the room, hostages were screaming, and the air resembled a fireworks display.

Beddoes saw a small boy start to run across the room, screaming for his mother, and she leaped up to intercept him. Suddenly she became aware of a burning sensation in her knee, and her leg buckled under her. She rolled once and tried to crawl toward the boy, screamed as her knee touched the ground, tried to slither toward a wall, felt a laser beam burn into her shoulder, screamed again, and lay perfectly still, eyes closed.

The madness went on around her for another four minutes, and then a human voice rang out: "The area is secured!"

The lights were turned on, and some fifty armed men and women began walking through the room. Half a dozen of them made sure that the Lodinites and jasons lying on the floor were truly dead, while the rest helped the hostages to their feet. Beddoes was one of four who couldn't rise, and a moment later the doctor was examining her and sealing the wound as best he could.

"Well?" asked McCreigh, coming over to join him.

The doctor shook his head. "Her knee's been blown off, and she's sustained a serious burn on her left shoulder."

"Will she live?"

"There's a burst artery here," said the doctor. "She's lost a lot of blood. She needs a transfusion, and she needs it pretty damned soon."

"What about the other three?"

"Two are mobile, one won't last out the hour."

"All right," said McCreigh. "Let me see the map."

"You have to take me with you!" mumbled Beddoes.

"You'll never make it," said McCreigh, studying a map someone had handed him. "We're going to drop you off at a hospital on the way to our ships."

"I'll take my chances," mumbled Beddoes. "Just get me out of here."

"You're already going into shock," said the doctor, injecting something in her arm. "Just lay back and try to relax."

"He'll kill me!"

"He won't lay a finger on you," said McCreigh. "Trust me."

She was about to ask him why she should trust him about anything, let alone her life, when the ceiling started spinning and everything went black.

Fifteen

Beddoes was aware of voices, some near, some distant, none of them speaking to her. Then she realized that the sun was shining on her face, and she turned her head away from it.

"I think she's coming around," said yet another voice. "Susan?"

"Go away," mumbled Beddoes.

"Susan, this is Arthur. Open your eyes."

Beddoes tried to reach her pillow to put it over her head; the pain of moving her arm was agonizing and severe, and suddenly she heard a scream. It took Beddoes a moment to realize that the sound had come from her.

"Welcome back," said another voice. "I thought we were going to lose you, for a while there."

She opened her eyes, flinched from the brightness of the sunlit room, and things slowly came into focus.

Arthur Cartright was sitting on a chair next to her bed, and Anton McCreigh was leaning lazily against a white wall.

"Where am I?" asked Beddoes.

"You're in the Boris Petrovitch Memorial Hospital in Remus," answered McCreigh. "Do you remember anything about how you got here?"

She closed her eyes again and concentrated. "I remember the rescue, and then everything goes blank." She paused. "Wait! I remember getting shot in the confusion. My shoulder, I think."

"Your shoulder was the least of your problems," said McCreigh.

"My knee!" she exclaimed, and then frowned. "I don't feel anything there."

"I'd be surprised if you did," said McCreigh. "We've got a brand new one on order for you."

"They *amputated* my leg?" she asked, horror-stricken.

"No choice," said McCreigh. "Even if they could have rebuilt the knee, the rest of your leg was hanging on by just a couple of threads of muscle. There was no way to get any blood circulating down there."

"I'm sorry, Susan," said Cartright. "You'd lost an enormous amount of blood; they were more concerned with saving your life."

"Besides, the new one will be prettier than the old one," added McCreigh lightly. "No varicose veins."

"How can you joke about it?" demanded Beddoes furiously. "I've just lost my leg!"

"You'd be surprised what they're doing with pros-
thetics these days," replied McCreigh.

"That's easy for *you* to say!" snapped Beddoes.

McCreigh smiled. "Easier than you think. Or
would you like me to remove my right arm for you?"
He held up the appendage, wiggling the fingers.
"Works better than the original."

"The doctors assure us that you'll be walking
within a few weeks, without any noticeable limp,"
said Cartright soothingly.

"I'll believe it when I see it," said Beddoes bitterly.

"Believe it," said McCreigh. "The current holder
of the three thousand and five thousand meter track
records is a fellow with two artificial legs. They're
trying to get him disqualified and his times disal-
lowed." He paused. "And now, if you're all through
thanking me for saving your life, is there anything
else you'd like to know?"

"I don't think much of your bedside manner,"
muttered Beddoes.

"Well, if push comes to shove, I don't think much
of your notion of 'Hit the deck,' " he answered
pleasantly.

"Why are you still here?" demanded Beddoes.

"Because of you," said McCreigh.

"Because of me?" she repeated, frowning.

"Someone in the Republic decided not to leave
you to the tender mercies of your President-For-
Life."

"She's very tired, and in obvious pain," said Cartright. "Perhaps we should let her go back to sleep. We can talk about this later."

"I'm all right," said Beddoes. "I want to hear about it *now*."

"Are you sure you feel strong enough?" asked Cartright solicitously.

"I'm sure, Arthur." She turned to McCreigh. "Tell me about the rescue. What happened?"

"It was a success," said McCreigh. "We lost two of our men and one hostage. Killed all fourteen Lodinites, and about a hundred and fifty innocent bystanders."

"Innocent bystanders?" said Beddoes. "I didn't see any."

"Oh, they were all wearing Faligor military uniforms, but President Labu swears they were bystanders," said McCreigh with a grin. "Anyway, except for you, all the hostages are on their way back to the Republic. You were in no condition to transport."

"You still haven't told me why you're here."

"We thought there was a possibility that Labu might take out his frustration on the one survivor, so I was ordered to remain behind until you've recovered."

"And you are expected to hold off the entire Faligor army?" said Beddoes in disbelief.

"Not at all," replied McCreigh. "I'm here as a representative of the Republic to inform them that any reprisals taken against one Susan Beddoes will be considered an act of war against the Republic, which will respond to such provocation with all the firepower at its command."

"I don't want to be the cause of a war," said Beddoes.

"You won't be," replied McCreigh with a smile. "Our position is totally illegal, and I doubt that we'd follow through if push came to shove. But Labu doesn't know that."

"You've just publicly humiliated him by swiping the hostages from right under his nose," noted Beddoes. "What makes you think that he'll leave me alone, despite your threats?"

"Because his army is busy elsewhere. Since he's afraid to go to war with the Republic, and the moles are all gone, he's busy decimating a tribe called the Chijanga this morning."

"The Chijanga are pastoralists who live a thousand miles from here, and never bother anyone," said Beddoes. "How did they get involved in this?"

"Probably because they're pastoralists who live a thousand miles from here and never bother anyone," replied McCreigh. "Labu went on the air again this morning. He claimed that the Chijanga were in collusion with the Republic, and that they helped free the hostages just when Labu had both sides poised on the verge of an agreement."

"In other words, he's wiping out an entire tribe just to save face?"

"That's about the size of it," agreed McCreigh.

"Okay, you've delivered your message," said Beddoes. "Why are you still here—and more to the point, why hasn't Labu thrown you in jail for participating in the rescue?"

"Two reasons," answered McCreigh. "First, he

was officially neutral during the crisis, and hence he can't favor one side over the other. Second, I've been attached to the Republic embassy, and while he probably doesn't know what diplomatic immunity means, he knows that you don't shoot embassy personnel.''

Beddoes turned to Cartright. "You know him better than I do, Arthur. He's not going to stop with slaughtering the Chijanga, is he?''

"I doubt it," said Cartright.

"How bad are things going to get?''

"Worse, I think, than either of us can imagine.''

It was an understatement.

Sixteen

After the rescue at the Remus spaceport, something seemed to snap inside Gama Labu's mind. Where before he had been cunning and barbaric, now he was merely bloodthirsty and barbaric. Where before he had at least made a pretense of governing in accordance with those laws that remained on the books, he now became a law unto himself. Where before those who had been dragged out of their houses and arrested in the middle of the night at least knew what their government had against them, now such arrests followed no comprehensible pattern.

When one of Labu's cabinet members was shot and killed in retaliation for the slaughter of a nearby village, Labu issued a proclamation allowing all government employees and members of the military to shoot anyone they felt might endanger their lives. This was immediately interpreted as the right to shoot anyone who voiced any opposition to any government policy.

At the same time, corruption ran rampant. Taxes were collected by whim, with many citizens being taxed five and six times a year. Any jason with an advanced degree who was still alive was drafted into the army and never seen again. Six more tribes vanished from the face of Faligor forever.

Rumors abounded about Labu himself. It was common knowledge that he was once again practicing the religion of his forebears, but those closest to him whispered that he had killed and eaten two of his wives at the urging of his witch doctor, who then disappeared, never to be seen again.

Another story told of Labu losing his courage on a hunting trip, when charged by a Plainstalker. Then, when his eldest son stepped forward and saved him by shooting the Plainstalker at point-blank range, Labu was said to have killed him and eaten his heart, convinced that his son's courage would now flow through *his* veins.

Where once one truck a day backed up to the Government Science Bureau, now they came and left by the hour, and the stench from the mass graves was omnipresent.

Any member of the government who aroused Labu's ire or jealousy was either replaced or simply vanished. As a result, the Treasury Department was run by a former printer's apprentice whose answer to everything was to print more money. The Interior Department decided that the best way to eradicate a flying insect that carried a disease that was fatal to the domestic livestock was to kill every wild animal that might carry the insect from one livestock herd to another; within three months they had slaughtered most of the remaining five million wild animals on the planet, without making an appreciable dent in the population of the flying insect. The head of the Patnet Bureau announced that there was nothing left to invent, closed its doors, and appropriated its funding for his personal use.

A few jasons and men still openly opposed the government. A group of eight religious leaders met with the President-For-Life to protest Labu's treatment of their followers; they were immediately arrested, and their anguished screams could be heard, night after night, throughout Romulus, until the last of them died eleven days later. A major in the army refused George Witherspoon's orders to set fire to his own village; he was stripped naked, covered with gasoline, and set ablaze. A jason doctor refused to stop tending to Labu's victims in a distant village; when word of his disobedience reached Labu, he was arrested and brought before the president, who filled one of the doctor's syringes with poison and injected it into him. Labu then ate a hearty meal while watching the doctor's agonized death throes.

One by one, the civilized races of the galaxy closed their embassies and withdrew their personnel. The first to leave were the Canphorites, followed by the Domarians, the Lodinites, the Mollutei, and finally the only embassy left functioning was the Republic, which had placed an economic embargo on Faligor but was unwilling to turn its back on the few remaining Men who still lived there.

Labu's reaction was simple and straightforward: he declared war on each of the departing races. He didn't have the means to make war on distant planets, but he methodically burned down each empty embassy and issued shoot-to-kill orders should any member of that race set foot upon Faligor for any reason.

Although entire embassies had closed, Labu never officially lifted his restriction on emigration, and as a result Beddoes remained on Faligor, her request for an exit visa being turned down more than a dozen times. It was as if the president realized that he could not kill her for attempting to aid the hostages, but he decided he could at least force her to spend the remainder of her days as a virtual prisoner on Faligor.

McCreigh remained too, certain that the moment he left Beddoes and probably Cartright would both be murdered. Eventually he bought a farm in the area, for lack of anything better to do. The first month he was there, his livestock was mutilated; the second month, his wells were poisoned; the third month, his house and barn were burned down, though he shot and killed seven of those responsible before they could flee. After that, he moved into the embassy compound, checking on Beddoes' situation every week or two, but taking no further interest in Faligor.

And despite all this, a few jasons still fought back. A Christian minister that the death squads had overlooked planted bombs in the Departments of Science and Agriculture, killing some four hundred government officials and leading Witherspoon a merry chase for the better part of three months before he was finally hunted down and tortured to death. Fifteen Enkoti females compiled a journal describing all the excesses of the past few years and managed, somehow, to smuggle it off the planet; Labu and Witherspoon never found out for sure who was responsible for it, but more than seven hundred Enkoti disappeared into the Government Science Building, never to emerge, during the attempt to learn the identities of the authors.

Perhaps the most successful rebellion was led by a schoolteacher named James Krakanna. When the army found out that he was criticizing the government to his young students, they sent a squad of twenty soldiers to arrest him. When the soldiers arrived, they were immediately mowed down by Krakanna and his "Children's Army," some fifteen jasons, none of them even adolescent, who had armed themselves with bows and poisoned arrows. They confiscated the dead soldiers' arms and disappeared into the dense forests encircling the Hills of Heaven, emerging when least expected to wipe out any of Labu's followers who were unlucky enough to cross their path. Within six months Krakanna's children numbered almost one thousand, all of them armed, and the threat became serious enough for Witherspoon to dispatch some fifty thousand troops to the Hills of Heaven to root them out. They found a few here and there, lost some three thousand of their own personnel, and finally decided that the operation wasn't worth the effort and went home. Krakanna promptly began launching his attacks once more.

Still, these were minor irritations to the President-For-Life, nothing more. His reign of terror continued unabated until two unrelated events occurred that, although no one knew it at the time, marked the beginning of his downfall.

First, with the last of his foreign currency spent on armaments, Labu found that he was unable to pay his army with anything but totally worthless Faligor dollars. The fifteen billion dollars that the average soldier made each week would no longer buy a single loaf of bread.

Second, he received word that William Barioke, who had been living in exile on neighboring Talisman ever since the coup, had been lobbying both the Talisman government and the Republic to overthrow Labu and restore him to power.

It was, Labu decided, a heaven-sent opportunity to get his army's mind off the fact that their astronomical salaries were worthless. He had amassed some sixty-three spaceships since assuming power. They all sat, fueled, fully-armed, and ready to fly, on the landing strip at the Remus spaceport. It seemed the perfect opportunity to put them to use, assuage his army, and replenish his empty coffers by plundering another planet.

The morning after he heard the rumors about Barioke, President-For-Life Gama Labu declared war on Talisman.

Seventeen

"You know," said Beddoes, sitting across the dinner table from Cartright, "this could be the best thing that ever happened to Faligor."

"How can you say that?" replied Cartright. "Nobody wins in a war."

"Nonsense, Arthur. That sounds great in a university lecture or a book, but the fact is that someone always wins. Who do you think writes the history books? The winners." She paused to take a bite of her food and swallow it. "I think Labu's in over his head this time."

"I don't know," said Cartright. "Talisman's economy is very little better than our own, and I don't remember anything about their having an effective military machine. I hope you're not counting on the Republic rushing to their aid; that ruler of theirs—that President Byamula—keeps turning down Man's overtures. More politely than Faligor, to be sure, but just as firmly."

"Look," said Beddoes, "it's populated by an alien race, and the Canphor Twins and Lodin XI and all the others are looking for allies against the Republic. The very fact that Byamula is under attack by a madman and the Republic *won't* help should mean that a few dozen other alien worlds will leap to his defense."

"And what if they do?" asked Cartright. "What then?"

"Then Gama Labu's days are numbered."

"So what? Talisman will take over Faligor, and we'll have another military dictatorship."

"Talisman can't afford to do that," said Beddoes. "It can barely afford to keep its own government in business."

"Maybe the combined outrage of the Republic and the alien planets will make Labu see reason," Cartright suggested hopefully.

"I don't know why you think it will," replied Beddoes. "Nothing else has."

"He's always played one side against the other," answered Cartright. "He's never really been in a position where *everyone* is against him."

"I doubt that he's losing any sleep over it," said Beddoes. "No, our best hope is for Talisman to form some quick alliances and decimate the invading forces."

"If it hasn't already fallen," replied Cartright gloomily.

"We're not talking about the Republic invading a planet with twenty million men and turning the sky black with battleships. These are two impoverished worlds, both ill-equipped for war on a planetary scale. It's not going to end that fast."

"But if Talisman gets the help it needs . . ."

"Moses Byamula is a proud man. He won't ask for help until he knows he needs it. That could take a day, or a week, or a month. Or maybe we're wrong, and he's capable of winning a war without any help at all."

"You make it sound like a problem in logic, Susan," said Cartright. "But it isn't—it's war. Right now it's taking place on Talisman, but if they fight off the invasion, the next battle will be fought here." He stared across the table at her. "Have you ever been in a war? I have, and take it from me, it's not pleasant."

"Neither is what's happened to Faligor since Labu gained power."

"That's for damned sure," agreed Cartright with a sigh. "Ah, well, there's no sense arguing about it. What will be, will be. Perhaps I should turn on the holo and see if we've received any news about it yet."

She stared at him and shook her head sadly. "Poor Arthur. You still think of this as the world you wanted it to be, rather than the world it is."

"I beg your pardon?"

"I'll tell you right now what the broadcasts will say. They'll say that we're winning victory after glorious victory, that we're advancing on the enemy and he is sustaining massive losses, that President Byamula has gone into hiding, and that victory is within our grasp." She paused. "They'll keep saying it right up to the moment that Byamula's forces land on Faligor and march into Labu's mansion.''

''Yes, I suppose they will. Still, it can't hurt to see what's on.''

He activated the holo, and true to Beddoes' prediction, the announcers predicted an imminent victory.

Then there was an insert of Gama Labu, stating that he personally abhorred war and would call it off as soon as Talisman agreed to surrender the traitor William Barioke to Faligor, and to pay the equivalent of two billion Republic credits as a penalty for harboring such a fugitive. Until Talisman's cowardly president met those two demands, the war would continue.

When the broadcast went back to offering obviously inflated counts of the enemy's losses, Cartright turned the set off.

''Surprised?'' asked Beddoes humorlessly.

''Puzzled.''

''Oh? What about?''

''Why doesn't Moses Byamula just turn Barioke over to us?''

''We also demanded extortion money to withdraw our army, remember?'' said Beddoes.

''I'm sure it's negotiable,'' answered Cartright. ''What Labu really wants is Barioke.''

''That's not so, Arthur. He also wants an external enemy, so people don't start looking at *him* when their money's no good and the electricity doesn't work and the water won't run.''

"All the more reason why Byamula should give Barioke to Labu. *I* would."

"Perhaps," said Beddoes dryly, "that's why you're not the president of Talisman."

Eighteen

Talisman was prepared for the attack. It had given refuge to literally tens of thousands of jasons, many of them government officials who had fallen from favor and had much information to trade in exchange for sanctuary.

Furthermore, Labu's ill-trained pilots were barely able to find Talisman, let alone their targets, and most of the initial rain of bombs fell into an ocean and onto an uninhabited desert. About half the weaponry Labu had purchased was in poor shape or else was incompatible with the ammunition he had bought for it.

The Talisman forces were no better equipped, but they *were* better trained, and within hours of the attack, more than half of Faligor's fleet had been decimated and the rest found itself fighting for its life.

Finally the commander of the flagship, a General Dushu, broke off his engagement and fled back to

Faligor, followed by the twelve surviving ships of his Navy, and the first phase of the war was over.

Moses Byamula, the President of Talisman, went before a meeting of the planetary heads of the Canphorite Federation, composed of some thirty-eight alien races, and asked for their support in his war against Gama Labu. The Federation went into private executive session, and emerged a few hours later with a statement condemning Labu's actions but stopping short of offering any tangible aid to Talisman.

Byamula next contacted the Republic, hoping for arms or money to pay for arms, and received only a similar statement of moral support.

Labu, for his part, was changing religions almost by the hour, looking for aid in exchange to his fealty to an alien god, but it was an old stunt and it didn't play well. Within days he was faced with the fact that almost every race in the galaxy had publicly condemned his act of aggression.

Hoping to save face, he offered a quick solution to the problem: Rather than risking further bloodshed on the battlefield, he proposed that Byamula—the leader of a race that averaged less than ninety pounds at maturity—meet him in the boxing ring, the victor to be declared the winner of the war as well.

Byamula's response was to launch a full-scale attack at Faligor. Realizing that his navy was not up to the kind of saturation bombing required for a quick and easy victory, he used them as transport ships, landing tens of thousands of his soldiers in the western desert. They secured the area, and every three days saw still more soldiers deposited there, until a substantial force had been assembled. They then turned to the east and began marching toward Remus. On those occasions that Labu's ill-trained forces met them in battle, the jasons were quickly defeated; more often, upon hearing of the Talisman Army's approach, the jasons simply threw down their arms and fled in the opposite direction.

Village after village turned out to greet the conquering army, to offer them food and encouragement and words of gratitude. By the time they were within a two-week march of Romulus and Remus, they had been joined by some thirty thousand jasons, many armed with nothing more than bows and arrows.

Labu soon realized that his army was not up to the task of halting the enemy, and he came up with the unique notion of bombing every jason village between the advancing army and Remus in the hope that the enemy would run out of food before they ran out of ground. The net result was eighty thousand jason casualties, and an enemy more convinced than ever that Right was on their side and that they had almost a sacred obligation to defeat Labu.

When they were camped forty miles outside of Remus, Labu ordered the burning of the Treasury and the Mint, so that his conquerors would find no money to loot—not that it was worth anything, anyway—and, under cover of night, he drove to his private spaceship, accompanied by George Witherspoon and three of his wives. Once there, he radioed his assurances to his army that he would soon be personally leading a counterattack, ordered his officers to shoot any deserters, and, as his last official act as President-For-Life, pulled a small pistol out of his belt and shot Witherspoon point-blank between the eyes.

By dawn, Labu was halfway to distant Domar, having once again converted to their ancient religion of Rainche.

Ninteen

The road to Remus was paved with flowers and corpses.

Talisman's army reached the city at noon, to the wild cheers of the populace, which had watched the rout of their own army some five hours earlier. The fighting continued for another three weeks, until the Talisman generals decided that the remnants of Labu's forces that had not yet been captured or surrendered offered no serious threat.

Journalists from all across the galaxy were allowed entry to Faligor, and finally the full extent of Labu's excesses became known. Some five thousand mass graves were unearthed, with the certainty that there were an equal number still to be found. The Government Science Center was dismantled after it was found to be the seven-story chamber of horrors that the locals suspected it to be. More than fifty dismembered jason bodies were found in the basement of the presidential mansion, while Labu's private quarters were stocked with children's games and picture books he had imported from the Republic over the years.

Finally, after order had been restored, Moses Byamula himself flew to Faligor, accompanied by William Barioke. Byamula announced to a gathering of more than one hundred thousand jasons in Remus that he was no conqueror, that he had no interest in administering the affairs of any world other than his own, and that his soldiers would return home as soon as the new government was once again in possession of the reins of power. He then concluded that his only official act was to return the duly-elected President of Faligor, William Barioke, to whom he had given sanctuary during Labu's reign.

Byamula then stepped aside, and Barioke, looking far older and much thinner than he had prior to his exile, walked up to a bank of microphones.

"The reign of terror has ended," announced Barioke to the wildly enthusiastic throng of jasons. "Gama Labu has been defeated, and Faligor's long nightmare has ended, never to return." The cheers were so loud that Barioke had to wait almost five minutes before he could make himself heard once more.

"Never again will jason be pitted against jason. Never again will an oppressed citizenry cringe in fear from the authorities who have been elected and appointed to serve them. Never again will jason infants grow up with the screams of the dying and the stench of the dead. A new day has dawned for

Faligor." He signaled to a jason officer, who was standing at attention. "You!" he said, and then pointed to the statue of Conrad Bland, that dominated the city center. "See to it that that statue is torn down before sunset!" Still more cheers. "I also want every park, every lake, every river, and every street that Gama Labu named after himself restored to their original titles."

"How soon will you want that done, sir?" asked the officer.

"Today," said Barioke firmly. "Tomorrow we've got a constitution to write and a planet to rebuild."

The applause was deafening, and though Barioke then left the platform to confer with his advisors, the celebration that followed continued well into the night.

III

SHARD

Interlude

You pass the ruins of a hospital, smell the charred bodies within, cover your nose, and keep walking.

And as you walk, you keep asking yourself: How could they not have learned? The whole galaxy knew about Gama Labu. Once the jasons got rid of him, how could they have let it happen again? Where were they when the torture chambers were rebuilt, the massive trenches filled once more with bodies?

These were intelligent people. They had to know what was happening, had to feel the same revulsion toward Labu that all sentient beings felt.

You look around at the smoldering ruins and shake your head in bewilderment. No civilized being wants to live like this. No civilized being, having undergone the totalitarian rule of a genocidal maniac, willingly accepts the yoke of another. Where was the opposition? Could it really have been just one schoolteacher and a handful of children?

And the moles? How could they fall for the same old line again? Even if the jasons hadn't learned, surely the moles could have seen what was coming. When you get away from the death and the destruction, is this planet so damned lovely that you leave all sense of self-preservation behind just to live here for as long as you can before they roust you out in the middle of the night and spirit you away to some torture chamber or mass grave?

An old jason sits in the entrance of a bombed-out store, staring at you with dull, lusterless eyes. You stare back at him, and while you wish he would smile, or wave, or do something besides just sit and watch you, you can hardly blame him. How many liberators has he welcomed, only to be betrayed by each in turn? And is there any reason to believe that the current one is any different?

Twenty

"But why *now?*" asked Cartright, truly puzzled, as he sat across the table from Susan Beddoes in a Remus restaurant. "We've finally gotten rid of him."

"Arthur, I never meant to stay," answered Beddoes. "I haven't been allowed to go until now."

He shook his head impatiently. "That's not what I mean." He paused, searching for the right words. "Don't you see? We've cut out Faligor's cancer. The planet is healthy again. Why leave now, when it's finally worth living here again?"

"That's *your* opinion," she replied.

"The land is still as fertile as ever," he persisted. "The climate is still the finest in the galaxy. With Labu gone, we'll be getting funding from everyone. The Republic is helping us to rebuild Romulus and Remus, the Canphorites have given us money to rebuild our roads, the Mollutei have offered to rebuild our medical clinics. It can be Paradise again."

"Arthur, it was *never* Paradise. The best that can be said is that it's no longer Inferno—at least for the moment."

"What do you mean, for the moment?" demanded Cartright. "Labu is through. He's hiding halfway across the galaxy. They'll never let him come back."

"Maybe everyone else on this planet has forgotten how happy you were when he took over," said Beddoes, "but *I* haven't." She paused and looked at him. "William Barioke was every bit as much a tyrant as Gama Labu. I see no reason to believe he's changed."

"How can you compare them? Look at the millions that Labu killed."

"He was in power a lot longer, that's all."

"Barioke has had years to dwell on his mistakes," said Cartright. "You've heard his speeches. I'm sure he's more moderate now."

"He's more moderate because all the galaxy is watching him," answered Beddoes. "Tell me what you think of him two years from now."

"Whatever he is, he's got to be better than Labu."

"Being better than Labu is like saying you have a medical condition that's better than terminal cancer," said Beddoes. "It's not exactly a ringing endorsement."

"Why haven't you mentioned your feelings about him before today?"

"Because I knew we'd just argue about it, and you're my closest friend."

"And there's no way you'll reconsider?" asked

Cartright plaintively. "Can't I convince you to stay just a few more months to see which of us is right?"

She shook her head. "Arthur, you're retired; I still have a living to make. I've lost a lot of income while I was forced to stay here."

"I can find work for you."

"I can find work for myself. Elsewhere." She paused again. "Look, Arthur, I came here many years ago to do a job for you, a job that was supposed to last for perhaps two or three months. I feel like I've spent half of my adult life on this planet. I've been virtually held prisoner, I've watched my friends disappear one by one. I've even lost a leg to this damned planet. Enough is enough."

"It's not a 'damned planet,' " insisted Cartright. "We've undergone a terrible ordeal, but it's over."

"I hope you're right," she said. "But this is your planet, not mine. You would stay here through ten Gama Labus, hoping for better. I don't have your emotional stake in it; I just want to get on with my life."

"You're making a mistake, Susan."

She shrugged. "If I am, it's mine to make."

He stared at her helplessly for a long moment. "When does your ship leave?"

"Tomorrow morning."

"And what will you do?"

"First I'll explain to my creditors why they haven't heard from me," she said with a smile. "And then I'll find out which colleges and museums are looking for an entomologist."

"Do you need money? I have an account back on Caliban. . . ."

She shook her head. "I thank you for the offer, but I didn't own much that could be repossessed."

"You'll keep in touch?"

"Of course I will."

"I'll drive you to the spaceport tomorrow."

"It's not necessary."

"It may be," answered Cartright. "That crazy Krakanna hasn't come in from the mountains yet. He sent word yesterday that he refuses to recognize Barioke as our President."

"Good for him," said Beddoes. "It's nice to know that someone on this planet understands what's happening."

"You're mistaken about him, Susan."

"Why? Because he remembers what Barioke was like the last time around?"

"Because he's still fighting a war while we're trying to secure a peace," answered Cartright. "And some of his statements are frightening."

"Why?"

"He doesn't believe in democracy, Susan."

"So far all democracy on Faligor has produced is William Barioke and Gama Labu," replied Beddoes. "I can't say that I blame him."

"I'm being serious," said Cartright.

"So am I. Maybe democracy doesn't work for every race and every world, Arthur."

"Of course it does. There was nothing democratic about the way Labu usurped power."

"From the duly elected president," she reminded him.

"I'll grant you that he wasn't a great president. . . ."

Beddoes laughed harshly.

"All right," conceded Cartright. "He wasn't even a good president. But he's got to have learned from his mistakes. And if not, we'll simply vote him out of office. That's what you do with bad presidents."

"No," said Beddoes. "That's what you do with incompetent presidents. Bad presidents usually have to be pried loose from the reins of power with a crowbar—or a revolution."

"Whatever he did, whatever he does this time, it won't be as bad as Labu."

Beddoes stared at him. "Arthur," she said at last, "you are a dear, sweet, decent man, and an idealist who sees only the best in others. Those are all exemplary qualities, and they're among the reasons that I'm so fond of you—but those very qualities also prevent you from seeing what is really happening right under your nose."

"You think so little of me?"

"I think the world of you, and I even have a certain fondness for Faligor—or at least for what it could have been," answered Beddoes. "That's why I don't want to be around for what happens next."

Twenty-one

A month into William Barioke's second presidency, Cartright was certain that Susan Beddoes was mistaken. The jason's first official act was to announce that elections would be held in six months' time. Within a week of taking office, he also invited the moles back to Faligor, and set up a commission to determine the damages owed each mole family that had been forced to leave the planet. Finally, he assembled a blue-ribbon panel to draft a new constitution, even including two moles and four men—Arthur Cartright among them—on the committee.

He emptied the jails of political prisoners and declared amnesty for any crimes committed during Gama Labu's reign. He publicly invited James Krakanna to come to the bargaining table, and promised that no reprisals would be taken against his army. (Krakanna refused, but the offer gained Barioke considerable public support.)

Cartright threw himself into his work on the new constitution, encouraged by Barioke's constant refrain that he wanted a constitution that would make tribalism impossible. It was only after five weeks of intensive work, when a draft of the document was presented to the president, that Cartright finally understood what the president meant: Barioke insisted that political parties would inevitably be divided along tribal lines, and demanded that his own party be the only legal one.

Cartright protested vigorously, but Barioke was adamant: allow twenty-four parties, he said, and the twenty-four remaining tribes (Labu had totally eradicated the three smallest) would each support one party. The only way to prevent this, argued Barioke, was to make all the tribes co-exist under the banner of a single political party.

His party.

Word of the president's intentions soon leaked out, protest marches were held, and within days thousands of Enkoti were arrested and incarcerated. The most vocal and popular of them were never seen again.

Barioke also declared that Labu's thugs could not be allowed to escape punishment for their crimes, and during his first two months in office he tried and convicted most of them for crimes against the state, a catchall term that included everything from breaking and entering to murder and high treason.

It wasn't long before Cartright realized that Barioke was going overboard on his quest for justice, trying and convicting tens of thousands of jasons who had only the remotest connection to Labu's government. Further, most of those being jailed were members of the Bolimbo and Traja tribes, traditional enemies of Barioke's own Rizzali tribe but unlikely employees or supporters of Labu.

Within three months Cartright realized that Barioke had no intention of accepting the constitution his committee had created, and finally resigned his post. Barioke summoned him to the rebuilt presidential mansion the next morning.

"Good morning, Arthur," said the lean, ascetic-looking jason as Cartright was ushered into his office.

"Good morning, Mr. President."

"Yesterday your resignation was delivered to me," said Barioke. "I had understood that we were making excellent progress on the constitution. What seems to be the problem?"

Cartright considered telling him the truth, but rejected the idea; Barioke, who unlike Labu had the support of most of the races of the galaxy, had no compunction about incarcerating and even executing Men, whereas his predecessor, bloodthirsty as he was, always drew a line between what he could do to his own people and what he could do to members of the human race.

"I have given the document my best efforts, Mr. President," answered Cartright. "I have nothing left to give, so I thought I would resign and let you replace me with someone who might have some fresh insights."

"I am refusing your resignation, Arthur," said

Barioke. "We need as many Men working on the constitution as possible, so that no one can say that it is an unfair document that favors jasons over Men. We are all Faligorians together."

"If you won't accept my resignation, Mr. President, can you at least tell me what displeases you about the document? If I knew why you refuse to present it to your congress for a vote, perhaps I might know what areas require more work."

"Certainly," said Barioke. "First of all, you still have not stated, in terms so forceful as to brook no opposition, that we are to be a one-party system."

"I beg your pardon, Mr. President, but it explicitly states in Section 8, Paragraph 17, that—"

"I know what it states," interrupted Barioke. "And I also know what it does not state. You must insert language to the effect that anyone attempting to form a rival party is guilty of treason and will be put to death."

"With all respect, sir, I find that unduly harsh."

"I find it absolutely essential."

"May I point out that had we not allowed multiple parties, you would not have been able to run against Emperor Bobby and win the presidency in the first place?"

"And it was Robert Tantram who undermined my presidency and made it possible for the maniac Labu to overthrow me," answered Barioke. "The language *must* be inserted."

"I will discuss it with my fellow committee members," said Cartright, "but I do not think that they will accept it."

"Then I will fire them and hire some who will," said Barioke. "In fact, I will start today by getting rid of the two moles."

"On what grounds, may I ask?"

"Arthur," said Barioke, "we want nothing more than to live in harmony with your race. You have given us money and education, you opposed Labu's illegal reign, you have always acted in our best interests." The jason paused, and his face seemed just a little more alien to Cartright. "But the moles are parasites. They bring nothing to Faligor. They do not work for Faligor's good, but for their own. We cannot give them the same rights as jasons and Men, or they will soon have an economic stranglehold on the planet." He stared at Cartright. "Labu was insane, but he had one good idea: get rid of the moles."

"You yourself invited them back, and have set up a commission to pay them damages," noted Cartright.

"I was mistaken," replied Barioke. "In fact, I dissolved the commission three days ago. I will not force them to leave by executive order, as Labu did, but if they are to stay, it cannot be as citizens of Faligor but as resident aliens. They must pay higher taxes, they must never be without their passports, they must receive permission to travel from one city to another. All this must be incorporated into our constitution, Arthur."

"Do you want these restrictions on all aliens, or just the moles?"

"On any aliens that the president considers to have a detrimental influence on Faligor."

"I'll speak to the committee," said Cartright.

"Please do."

"Is that all?"

"No," said Barioke. "There is one more thing we must address."

"Yes?"

"We are a poor planet, Arthur, and Labu's reign has destroyed our economy. I would be a poor president indeed if I allowed us to be plundered any farther."

"*Is* someone trying to plunder us, Mr. President?"

"Not consciously, perhaps, but yes, someone is," answered Barioke. "Our constitution must make it clear that it is a criminal offense for any Man or mole who resides upon Faligor and carries a Faligorian passport to possess any investments or bank accounts on any other world. We cannot allow you to make your money here and invest it elsewhere."

"Does this law apply to jasons as well?" asked Cartright, who like everyone else was aware of Barioke's huge accounts on Talisman.

"No jason would consider removing his money from Faligor," answered Barioke. "This law will apply only to naturalized citizens."

"Since no jason would consider it, we might as well include them too," said Cartright. "Just in case one of them should consider it in the future."

Barioke shook his head. "I have no personal objection, Arthur," he said. "But various members of the legislature might take offense at such language, and we want the constitution to pass unanimously."

He paused and stared at Cartright coldly. "I think you had better word it just as I said."

Cartright sighed. "Yes, Mr. President."

"Good," said Barioke, rising from his chair. "I am glad to have you back on the team, Arthur."

"Thank you, sir," said Cartright, who could not bring himself to reply that he was glad to *be* back on the team.

"I know you and I disagree on many issues," continued Barioke, "but we both want what is best for Faligor. I am sure we can continue working together. This committee needs Men on it."

Tokens, you mean, thought Cartright.

"I am sorry I don't have more time to spend with you," said Barioke, walking him to the door, "but I have a meeting scheduled with my military advisors." He grimaced. "This Krakanna and his schoolchildren have actually had the audacity to print and distribute a newspaper containing the most slanderous lies about me. I've been too busy trying to rebuild the government to pay him any attention, but this latest exploit is intolerable. I won't rest until he has been arrested, tried and executed." He paused and forced a smile to his golden lips. "But that needn't concern you, Arthur. Just keep working on the constitution. You will find that I have ways of thanking my friends for jobs well done."

Cartright left the office, knowing that he would never present Barioke with the constitution the president wanted, and wondering just how he rewarded his enemies.

Twenty-two

Dear Susan:

As you must have guessed from my recent letters, things are not working out here. During the past three years, Barioke has proven to be everything you said he was. I was as blind to it initially as the rest of the populace: we were so glad to have someone, anyone, other than Gama Labu that we virtually turned over the whole world to him, without quite remembering why we had had such high hopes for Labu in the first place.

His approach is totally different from Labu's, and no one will ever accuse him of being a madman, but I have a horrible fear that the body count will be even higher under Barioke than under Labu. More than a million Labu "supporters" have been executed—and as you and I both know, the only true Labu supporters were the soldiers that he paid.

I served on the constitution committee for a few months, although it was clear to me early on that Barioke wanted a document that was a constitution in name only. Evidently, while my committee continued to work on the document, he created a committee of his cronies to write a constitution as well, and that is the one that has been ratified. Essentially, it gives Barioke the freedom to loot, plunder and kill as he pleases, with the full force of the law behind him. (I am reminded that neither Hitler nor Bland ever officially broke the law, either. They killed the lawmakers and rewrote the laws.)

For example, two weeks ago the teachers at Sabare University went on strike after he cut their pay and raised the salaries of the military. He had almost three hundred of them shot down in the street, and then announced that our new constitution makes it a capital crime to strike against any government-owned institution. And except for the small shops and markets, the government—which means William Barioke—owns just about everything else.

Why do the people support him? I don't know. Perhaps we used up most of our energy and most of our martyrs opposing Gama Labu—or perhaps they're willing to settle for anything after Labu. He wiped out a generation of jasons, including almost all of the intellectuals, and what's left simply can't seem to mount any effective opposition to his successor.

Oh, there are a few jasons, here and there, who oppose his rule, though I hardly find them comforting. The most persistent—and dangerous—of them all is James Krakanna, who is still hiding out in the forests around the Hills of Heaven. His typical "soldier" is a twelve-year-old jason subadult, armed with a laser or sonic rifle that weighs half as much as the subadult does. It's absolutely terrifying to think of these children, totally without family or discipline, wandering the countryside, robbing the locals of food, being unable to differentiate friend from foe and firing at anything that moves. They fight for this radical leader who time and again has spoken out against the most basic democratic principles.

The crazy part is that the people out in the countryside continue to give Krakanna aid and comfort. He and his "army" have been living off the land for close to two years now, and no one has turned him in yet, even though there is evidence that he and some of his advisors—whether children or adult, I don't know—have spent an occasional evening in the locals' homes. Barioke has his flaws, Lord knows, but there is at least a chance we can work with him and control some of his worst impulses. There seems to be absolutely nothing anyone can do to moderate Krakanna's actions, or make him bring in his impoverished, ragtag army for assimilation and retraining.

He has launched a number of attacks against the government, most of them successful. He has wiped out two expeditionary forces sent to hunt him down, and though not an Enkoti himself, has received vigorous support from them by making almost all Enkoti territory from the mountains to about fifty miles west of Romulus and Remus unsafe for any member of the government.

These attacks have not been without their share of casualties among Krakanna's forces. I have seen the torn, twisted bodies of jason children on the battlefields, and I cannot help but wonder what kind of monster sends children out to fight his battles. They're practically babies, Susan, and yet he keeps sending them out to face Barioke's army.

Then, at the other end of the spectrum, there are the

remnants of Labu's army. Once they found out that Bari-
oke's declared amnesty was false and that he was in fact
executing anyone who had anything to do with Labu's
government, the army—what was left of it, anyway—
began gathering in the Great Northern Desert. Rumor has
it that their leader is General Sibo Dushu, the very same
officer who led the retreat when Talisman mounted its first
counterattack. They haven't presented much of a threat
yet, but you can be sure that they won't surrender or trust
Barioke's word. And, since they are in Bolimbo country,
they are being supplied with food, money and even weap-
ons by the Bolimbo, who have no reason to love President
Barioke. He has excluded them—in fact, he has excluded
everyone except the Rizzali—from serving on his cabinet.

So that's the situation. Left to his own devices—and I
don't see anything standing in his way except Dushu's
army or Krakanna's children, neither of which constitutes
an improvement—I think there is every likelihood that
Barioke will kill more of his own people, coldly, methodi-
cally, but legally, than Labu ever did. The economy is still
in a shambles, most of the moles who have come back are
considering leaving once more, and the farms lie fallow
and untended, for there are so many opposing forces here
that most farmers are afraid that they'll be killed, or at
least looted, by one side or the other if they work their
fields.

Once again I find myself wondering how such a promis-
ing world, filled with such decent, hard-working, and
trusting inhabitants, could find itself in this situation. Is
it simply that Faligor expended all its energy and resources
surviving the Labu era, that there's simply no energy, no
will left to oppose Barioke's abuses? Or is there something

inherent in the jasons? They don't seem like sheep to me, but possibly I'm prejudiced.

Are they born victims? I have to believe they aren't, simply because I, too, welcomed both Labu and Barioke with open arms, and I know that Men aren't born victims. I keep asking myself what a planet of Men would do in this situation. I've gone through the history books looking for answers, but I can't seem to find an analogous situation. Yes, the Germans welcomed Hitler, but they were suffering from economic ruin caused by the Treaty of Versailles. Yes, the Romans accepted Caligula, but he did not hold an elective office and did not overthrow an existing government; indeed, during his four-year reign, he was officially declared a god. Conrad Bland? He was an executioner gone mad, but he never attempted to control a world; his specialty was destroying them.

I cannot find an example of a prosperous, well-run nation, bound by laws, happily welcoming anything resembling a Gama Labu. In every such case, it was a world or a society on the ropes, an economy in such chaos that people willingly (or occasionally unwillingly) gave up some or all of their rights in exchange for the promise of prosperity and stability. That, I might add, is not the promise Labu gave them, not really . . . but it is the promise Barioke made when he was reinstalled, so perhaps that much is understandable. It is when you put the two of them together, back to back, that you wonder if this entire world isn't somehow mad.

And yet I persist in believing that it is not, that it was a chain of unique circumstances that led to the current situation. Bobby lost the election because he was too close to Men, too much like us, and because he refused to take his opposition seriously—and the nature of his flaws logically led to an opponent who opposed his tilt toward Men and the Republic. If Bobby wanted to be a human, and many jasons think he did, then the opposition would naturally court other races and empires. If Bobby thought our legal principles were paramount, then the opposition would of course challenge each and every one of them. If Bobby was born a sitate and spent his money profligately, then his opposite number would be born a peasant and would not only save his own money, but would be inclined to plunder from a seemingly bottomless planetary treasury. It may well be that, under the circumstances, a William Barioke was inevitable.

That leads to the next question: given Barioke, was Gama Labu also inevitable? How can a madman, a fluke to begin with, be inevitable?

The answer, I think, is not that Labu himself was inevitable, but the circumstances that led to his usurpation of power made an overthrow of the government inevitable. You have a young, strong, new society that has just had its first election, and finds itself with a corrupt, bigoted ruler on its hands. They've had no experience with voting rulers out of office, and they've progressed so rapidly that a five-year presidential term seems like an eternity, so naturally somebody, somewhere, was going to consider forcefully removing Barioke from office. Who better to do so than the man in charge of the military? At least he does so with the knowledge that the army won't oppose him. And because it's a bloodless coup, and he promises the people that he has no intention of ruling but will arrange for a new election, of course they welcome him with open arms. That the head of the military took over makes sense; that the head of the military happened to be Gama Labu was the fluke.

After Labu's abuses, after the torture and slaughter, the mindless killings, the near-deification not only of Labu but of Conrad Bland, the greatest genocidal maniac in human history, of course the people were thrilled to welcome Labu's replacement, whoever it might be. I was just as happy to welcome Barioke as everyone else. Who else had any experience in running the planet? And why shouldn't we have assumed that he'd spent his years in exile dwelling upon his failed presidency and the reasons for his overthrow? His initial speech even addressed the subject: he knew he'd made mistakes, and he would learn from them. He knew that if he could be deposed once for abusing his power, it could happen again. He knew he was on probation of a kind. He'd already stockpiled millions of Republic credits in his account at Talisman, so how much more could he want?

That leaves only the question of why no one, or almost no one, has opposed him. I don't know. I do know that he's firmly entrenched, and that his military is totally loyal to him. The only way to remove him from power that I can see is through revolution. No other planet will involve itself in our affairs, barring a crazed impulse on Barioke's part to attack one of our neighbors—and he knows what happened when Labu did it—so I think if he falls, it will be at the hands of either Sibo Dushu or James Krakanna. One of them is a Labu loyalist who proved incompetent to lead his ships into battle and has had no experience in land wars, and the other is a teacher with a handful of children at his disposal.

Further, even if one or the other should manage to

overthrow Barioke, I'm not sure we'd be any better off. We certainly don't want to be ruled by a Labu loyalist, one who might even consider recalling Labu himself from Domar, and Krakanna is a radical who sees children as nothing but cannon fodder.

More and more often, I find myself thinking back to that first day I landed on Faligor. It was such a beautiful, tranquil world, and it held such promise, and I cannot help but wonder: was it always destined to become such a charnel house? Did we merely hasten the process, or did we cause it? If we had left it alone, if Bobby were sitting in the dirt today, making judgments in front of his mummified ancestors, would Faligor be better off? Would Gama Labu be killing his countrymen by twos and threes and fives, rather than hundreds and thousands?

Is the flaw in them, or in my vision?

I have done everything I can to convince myself that everything that happened was inevitable, and I think it was, with one exception: it was not inevitable that we landed here and attempted to turn it into Paradise. Nowhere is it written in the Book of Fate that Arthur Cartright had to impose his values on a peaceful, happy people who never knew or cared that he existed until the day he decided to shape their society to his vision of utopia.

I wish I were a religious man, because I feel the need to ask forgiveness of someone, and I cannot face the jasons to ask for theirs.

Love,
Arthur

Twenty-three

Unlike his predecessor, when William Barioke got angry, he didn't rant and rave and cry for blood. He became even more quiet, more distant, more in control of himself. He never raised his voice and he never lost his temper—but woe betide the jason who had caused his wrath.

He summoned his cabinet in the middle of the night, and when the last of them arrived, bleary-eyed and worried—for members of his cabinet had been known to be executed for failing to obey the law as interpreted by the president—he stood before them, waving a sheet of paper.

"I have just been informed that the Republic has cut off all aid to Faligor," he said in cold, measured tones. "They have ordered all their ships to avoid landing here, and they will not allow any Faligorian ship to land on any Republic world."

"What is the cause of this betrayal of our friend-

ship and good will?'' demanded one of his aides,
quite certain that the president was about to tell
them, but wanting to get his own outrage on record
first.

"They claim to have a list of some 643 documented abuses of the rights of individual jasons and
moles, and they have accused the government of
misappropriating funds," replied Barioke.

This caused considerable uneasiness among the
cabinet members. The logical response would be to
jump up and steadfastly deny the charges, but since
everyone knew them to be true, and in fact an understatement, they simply sat still, waiting for the president's next words.

"These charges were made and documented by
James Krakanna," continued Barioke. He spoke very
softly, very slowly, but in the total silence of the
room no one had any difficulty hearing him. "This
schoolteacher and his ragtag followers have ceased
to become an irritant, and are now a serious threat to
our government." The president paused and looked
from one cabinet member to the next. "I want Krakanna dead and his followers all killed or in prison
within a month. I will accept no excuses." Barioke
walked to the door. "I will leave the details to you,
and I strongly advise you not to fail me."

Then he was gone, leaving his ministers to cope
with the problem.

Twenty-four

Within ten days of the cabinet meeting, some four hundred thousand troops marched out of Remus toward the Hills of Heaven with a single purpose: to kill James Krakanna and destroy his army.

They spent twenty days combing the countryside looking for any trace of Krakanna and his followers, and finding none. The local villages denied having any knowledge of his whereabouts; a few went so far as to disclaim any knowledge of Krakanna's existence. It was a twenty-day exercise in futility, broken only by the screams of the dying as the army marched over a dozen widely-dispersed and well-hidden minefields.

True to his word, Barioke dismissed every cabinet member from office thirty days after the meeting. Some were merely exiled; most disappeared, never to be seen again. The president, convinced that the villagers had lied to his soldiers, ordered every village they had visited to be destroyed as an example to any other jasons who might be inclined to protect Krakanna.

Krakanna remained invisible for the better part of two months, then launched a series of attacks on widely-dispersed and poorly-protected government and military outposts, adding appreciably to his munitions in the process. Word filtered through to Remus that his ragtag army was growing larger every day.

Barioke sent out another huge column of soldiers to find him, and Krakanna lured them further and further into the dense rainforests, then attacked individual units that had become separated from the main body of troops, and kept fighting his guerilla war until the army had to retreat.

Barioke discovered that Krakanna was a member of the Trajava, a tribal subgroup of the Traja, and sent his army off to kill as many Trajava as it could find. More than a quarter of a million of Krakanna's tribesmen died before the few survivors were so dispersed that the army decided it was counterproductive to pursue them further.

Krakanna bided his time. Then, in an audacious nighttime raid, he and some of his followers snuck into Remus and destroyed the entire fleet of twenty-nine spaceships, retreating before anyone realized they had ever been there.

Barioke offered enormous rewards for any information leading to Krakanna's capture. Not a single jason stepped forward, and in retaliation, Barioke announced that he would destroy one village a day, without regard to tribe or location, until Krakanna surrendered himself to the army in Remus. Krakanna sent a reply, never made public, that he would kill ten soldiers and two government officials for every jason that Barioke killed.

Barioke determined that the message had come from the rainforest surrounding the Hills of Heaven, and mobilized his entire army. Within four days the forest was totally surrounded, and the president gave the order to begin tightening the noose. All lines of communication with the outside world were cut off, all means of egress were closed, and the army began methodically dividing the enormous forest into manageable sections, thoroughly searching one before moving on to the next.

It was sound strategy, and it might have worked, given enough time.

But time was one thing William Barioke did not have. With his army occupied two thousand miles away, Romulus and Remus were defended by only a token force, and General Sibo Dushu, taking full advantage of the situation, swept down from the Great Northern Desert with the remnants of Gama Labu's army and took control of the twin capitals in less than a day.

Barioke was marched out in manacles to the city center, where the statue of Conrad Bland had once stood, and was publicly executed.

Dushu then announced that he would be happy to share power with Krakanna, invited him to come to Remus and help form a new government, vowed

to transfer Barioke's private funds to the Faligor treasury, and insisted that the press sit in on every meeting he had, so that the populace would know that he
wasn't just another in the line of egomaniacal dictators, but truly had the planet's best interests at heart.

Arthur Cartright was standing in the crowd that
had gathered to hear Dushu speak. Though he still
hoped for the best, and applauded politely at the
proper points in the speech, this time he decided not
to join the frantic cheering that followed the pro-
nouncements.

IV

DUST

Interlude

Y ou climb the scorched steps of the Parliament building, and when you reach the top, you stop and turn
and look out on the broad thoroughfare, now littered with
bodies. Gama Labu looked down from here once, and
William Barioke, and Sibo Dushu, and you wonder what
they saw? Was it cheering faces and a hopeful future that
somehow went awry, or did they just see golden sheep, ripe
for the slaughter?

There are no cheering throngs this time, no hopeful
citizens lining the streets, no bureaucrats ready to rubber-
stamp whatever the newest conqueror wants. There are just
the dying and the dead, and the hungry avians circling
overhead, as they once used to circle over the kills in the
game parks.

You hear a noise behind you and turn to find an elderly
jason, his clothing soaked with blood, staggering toward
you. You go to him, catch him just before he collapses, and
help ease him down to the marble flooring.

He opens his mouth and rasps out a word. It is in a dialect you do not understand, but you know he is asking for water, and you open your canteen and hold it to his lips. He takes two swallows, then leans back and looks up at you gratefully.

"Do you speak Terran?" you ask. "Are there any more of you inside?"

But he is unconscious now, and you enter the building, your footsteps echoing through the still, dead air. And as you walk you ask yourself why you are bothering. Worlds have traditions: for some it is industry, for others agriculture or art. But for Faligor the tradition is genocide.

You are only halfway through your search of the building when you hear your name being called, and you thankfully return to the sunlight. Your team has found five more survivors, all children, and you clamber down the stairs and prepare to go to work, wondering all the while if you are merely saving them for the next maniac to come along. . . .

Twenty-five

Sibo Dushu didn't break his promises. In fact, he referred to them every day. He simply found it necessary to put them off until he could restore order—and since he had an army at his disposal, the restoration of order did very little to endear him to the populace.

He announced a curfew for every city under his control, and gave his soldiers shoot-to-kill orders for anyone breaking that curfew. Unfortunately for his public image, the first four people shot were two ambulance drivers, a doctor, and a patient who was being rushed to a Romulus hospital after dark.

That public image wasn't enhanced when a member of the Thosi tribe tried to assassinate him. Before anyone could work up much sympathy or outrage, his reprisal left more than two hundred thousand Thosi dead.

Since Faligor's money was still worthless, Dushu

announced an innovative new tax: his soldiers would perform a methodical house-to-house (and hut-to-hut) search for items that could be sold for hard currency on those few worlds that were still willing to have commerce with Faligor. The penalty for refusing the search was death, and the penalty for not producing something worthwhile for the searchers was death or imprisonment, depending on the mood of the searchers. This instantly halved the unemployment rate in the cities and created an entirely new field of widespread endeavor: thievery. Jasons robbed their neighbors, their stores, even their museums, in order to have something to give the soldiers when their domiciles were visited.

At the same time, Dushu kept calling upon James Krakanna to surrender his arms and join him at the conference table. Krakanna replied that any soldier or government employee who wandered more than thirty miles to the west of Remus would be shot on sight. Dushu wasn't much of a general, but he knew more about military tactics than Barioke, and he realized that he couldn't ferret out an entrenched guerilla army from the rainforest, so he settled for alternately threatening Krakanna and entreating him to join in the formation of the new government.

As Krakanna grew bolder and his raids more successful, Dushu became obsessed with him. Everyone knew that Krakanna's army was growing almost by the hour, but no one knew how large it was, how well-equipped it was, or even what Krakanna's eventual goals were. The new president ignored all the other problems facing him and concentrated on drawing Krakanna out into the open. Entire cities went without water and without power, roads went unpaved, even the spoils of his new "tax" remained in warehouses rather than being sold for hard currency.

As weeks passed and Dushu was still unable to obtain any information about Krakanna's strength or position, he concluded that an all-out attack was imminent, and pulled his army back to fortify Romulus and Remus. Any cities or villages that were loyal to him would have to fend for themselves; until he knew the size of the force he would be facing, he couldn't spare a single soldier for any of them.

Krakanna was silent for a week, then two weeks, then a month, and the tension in Romulus and Remus grew with each passing hour. Nervous soldiers shot each other in the night, supporters of Dushu locked themselves inside their homes, and Dushu himself went nowhere without an elite bodyguard of forty jasons.

Then, finally, Krakanna broke his long silence but not to Sibo Dushu.

Twenty-six

Dear Susan:
       Something has to be done. Dushu's reign promises
to be even bloodier than the last two, difficult as that must
be for you to comprehend. He's a disciple of Gama Labu,
and he's taken over a world that has been so decimated
and plundered by his predecessors that there is almost no
opposition to him. The jasons have been beaten down,
physically and spiritually, and can offer only token resis-
tance.

       There is only one hope for Faligor. I hesitate to suggest
it, since I have so long opposed him, but James Krakanna
is still out there in the forest, and rumor has it that his
army is growing larger every day.

       I mention this only because I received a curious letter,
ostensibly asking me to meet with him. I cannot be sure of
its authenticity, nor do I know why he should want to see
me, but something has to be done, and so I have agreed.

       His emissary is due to arrive momentarily. How we will

*make it through Dushu's lines to Krakanna's encamp-
ment I do not know, but I suppose if the emissary makes
it to my house, there must be a way.*

*I have serious reservations about this meeting, but the
alternative is to do nothing, and I have done nothing for
too many years now. I cannot sit idly by and watch this
planet raped and plundered a third time.*

*If you do not hear from me again, you will know that
I was mistaken once again, but at least I died trying to
help this once-beautiful world that I still love.*

Love,
Arthur

Twenty-seven

It took Cartright and his guide two days to make their way through Dushu's lines and into the massive forest that surrounded the Hills of Heaven. Cartright didn't see a single soldier, though he was certain that hundreds of them were watching as they progressed deeper and deeper into the forest.

Finally the road ended, and they got out of their vehicle and left it behind. Since the guide seemed confident that there was no need to lock or hide it, Cartright didn't suggest that he do so.

They walked along a rough dirt path for a few miles, with Cartright stopping to rest every half hour.

"Is something wrong?" asked the guide after the fourth halt.

"No," said Cartright, leaning against the thick bole of a tree and trying to catch his breath. "I've just realized that I'm not as young and fit as I used to be."

The guide accommodated him by slowing the pace, and at noontime they came to an encampment in the midst of a large clearing. There were some fifteen tents, including a huge one that Cartright assumed must be Krakanna's. A number of jasons, some of them adult, most adolescents, were going about their chores, cleaning weapons, gathering firewood, policing the grounds.

Two small jason boys, both armed, were squatting down playing a game that involved a number of sticks and pebbles; when they saw Cartright, they immediately stood up and saluted. Cartright smiled at them, then realized as they remained rigid and motionless that they were waiting for him to return their salute. He did so, one of them smiled at him, and they went back to their game.

He was then ushered into a large tent, and he found himself face-to-face with a small, wiry, middle-aged jason who stood up to greet him.

"I am James Krakanna," he said, extending his hand. "I am very glad you decided to come, Mr. Cartright."

"I'll be very blunt with you, Mr. Krakanna," said Cartright, taking his hand. "You have done many things of which I disapprove. But you are opposed to Sibo Dushu, and for that reason alone, it would have been criminally irresponsible for me not to at least listen to what you have to say."

"Fair enough," said Krakanna. "I admire your honesty."

"To the best of my knowledge, we have never met

before," continued Cartright. "May I ask why you have sought me out?"

"We have never before met as equals," replied Krakanna, "but I have seen you many times. You were an important force in Faligor's history, Mr. Cartright, and now you are one of the last Men on the planet." He paused. "Our recent history is as much your doing as anyone's, and I thought you might like to help set things right."

"Now just a minute . . ." began Cartright heatedly.

"I make no accusations," interrupted Krakanna. "I place no blame. I do not question your love for Faligor. I only point out that prior to Man's attempts to shape us into your version of Utopia, there was no carnage, there was no genocide, there was no Gama Labu or William Barioke or Sibo Dushu."

"We never meant for them to abuse their power," said Cartright.

"I know that. And yet they *have* abused it. The three of them have killed off very close to a third of our population. They have destroyed our economy, destroyed the fabric of our society, and alienated those worlds that might have been our friends. This is why I continue to wage war."

"With children," said Cartright disapprovingly.

"Look around you, Mr. Cartright," said Krakanna. "All that's left are children."

Cartright sighed deeply and considered the statement. "All right, Mr. Krakanna," he admitted. "You have a point."

"Please sit down, Mr. Cartright," said Krakanna, taking a chair for himself and indicating an empty one to Cartright, who gratefully walked over and sat on it. "I didn't send for you to make points, but to ask for your help. I am going to launch my attack on Dushu in about a month. I have bided my time, waiting until I knew there were no more tyrants lurking in the background. As far as I can tell, he is the last, and so my battle shall be with him. We will win, Mr. Cartright, but at enormous cost in life to both sides."

"How do I know you won't become just another tyrant after you win?" said Cartright, gratefully accepting a tall glass of water from an aide who entered the tent.

"You don't," replied Krakanna. "But you have free run of my camp, and I will see to it that you are given free passage to any area that is under my control. You may ask questions of anyone you encounter—soldier, villager, nomad, it makes no difference—and I will instruct your escorts to let you ask those questions in private. Before you leave, I want you to satisfy yourself that what I tell you now is the truth."

"That seems fair."

"It is essential that I be fair with you, Mr. Cartright," he said, "because I am going to make you do something you have never done before: I am going to make you choose between two sides and support one of them."

"I support whatever is best for Faligor," said Cartright.

"Empty words, Mr. Cartright. It is time for you to

stop being a passive observer, and join the forces of Good against those of Evil. It is that simple."

"Nothing is ever that simple," said Cartright.

"This is," answered Krakanna forcefully. He paused for a moment, as if trying to order his thoughts. "I want you to know," he continued, "that not a single one of my followers has ever been paid so much as a single credit in salary, and yet we have not had any deserters in more than four years."

"How do they live?"

"The same way we lived before you came to Faligor: off the land."

"How large is your army?" asked Cartright.

"Large enough for the task at hand. I also want it noted that we have never killed any moles or Men, and the only jasons we have killed have been those wearing the military uniforms of Barioke or Dushu, nor will we kill Dushu when we capture Remus."

"How can I prove that to my satisfaction?" asked Cartright. "Your soldiers will almost certainly support your statements."

"Ask any villager you come across. Offer my soldiers money to contradict what I have said. You are an intelligent being, Mr. Cartright; you will find ways to determine whether or not I am telling the truth."

"All right," said Cartright. "Let me grant for the moment that everything you have said is true. What does that have to do with me? I still don't know why you wanted to see me."

"I have been observing you for years, Mr. Cartright," said Krakanna, "and I have come to the conclusion that you are an honorable man. Not a practical or a realistic one, but an honorable one, which is sufficient for my purposes." He paused again, while Cartright tried to decide whether he had just been complimented or insulted. "The few doctors that were not killed by Labu and Barioke work in the cities; we do not have any medical personnel with our army. Our medical supplies, by which I mean those we have stolen, are minimal, and I suspect Dushu will destroy his own once he realizes that the battle is lost and my troops will soon be occupying both Romulus and Remus. Dushu has gathered all his troops around the two cities and this promises to be the bloodiest battle ever fought on this planet. A good many of the wounded on both sides will need expert medical attention, and this is where you come in."

"How?" asked Cartright.

"I want you to become our representative to the Republic, and to urge them to arrive with medics and supplies after we launch our final attack. Their presence here could save literally thousands of jason lives—on both sides."

"I'm surprised you care what happens to your enemies," said Cartright.

"There is a difference between necessary killing and senseless slaughter, Mr. Cartright," replied Krakanna. "And unlike my predecessors, I do not plan to unite this planet by killing off every last jason who disagrees with me. In case it has escaped your notice, it's been tried before without much success."

He paused. "Well, Mr. Cartright, on which side do you stand?"

"I'm not sure yet," answered Cartright. "I like what I have heard, but I have been fooled before." He stared at Krakanna. "Why are you on record as opposing a democratic form of government?"

"I oppose it at this point in time because the general populace's lack of literacy and the sad state of communications—radio, video, holo, newspaper—make it impossible for more than a small percentage of us to cast an informed vote."

"And the alternative is to install yourself as dictator?" asked Cartright dryly.

"I have no intention of being a dictator," replied Krakanna. "There are many forms of government other than democracy and tyranny, Mr. Cartright. Your racc's home planet offers numerous examples, ranging from monarchy through republic through socialism and communism. Your African nation of Botswana had a popularly-elected president and lower house of the legislature, while the upper house was composed entirely of hereditary tribal chiefs."

"You seem to have studied us very thoroughly."

Krakanna smiled. "I was a teacher of political science before I became a guerilla leader. I have fond hopes of returning to that profession someday."

Cartright stared at him for a long moment.

"If you can convince me you are telling the truth," he said, "I will do whatever I can to help you."

Twenty-eight

Dear Susan:

    I have been to see James Krakanna, and I have come away convinced that he is the one jason who can save this beleaguered world.

    I know, I know, I've said that before about other leaders, but this time I'm sure that I'm right. We spoke for many hours, and while I do not wholly approve of his politics or his methods, they were both shaped by the events that I helped to trigger through my ignorance and my idealism. Even an old man can learn from his mistakes, and I think I am learning from mine.

    Krakanna claims that he has no desire to rule Faligor, that he wants to reinstate the original constitution and hold elections within three months of forcing Dushu out of office. I've heard that before from every other leader, and I must confess that while I think he believes it, I don't foresee it happening. Nor would it necessarily be a good thing: Krakanna has too much to offer to go back to being *a schoolteacher. There probably aren't twenty jasons left alive with the equivalent of a college education; Faligor can't afford not to make use of each of them.*

I spent almost two days as Krakanna's "guest," going where I pleased and speaking to whomever I pleased, and I rid myself of a number of misconceptions. For example, while I have been calling this a children's army for quite some time, well over half its members are battle-hardened adults, and they're in command of most of the units. But it's the children that you see and the children that you remember. During the time I was there I saw literally thousands of them. Most were undernourished, some were unarmed, very few of them spoke or understood Terran, but all of them were unfailingly friendly and polite—and most of them had been in combat.

I stopped to speak to some of them, and inevitably their stories were the same: their families, and frequently their entire villages, had been destroyed by Labu or Barioke or, in the case of the most recent recruits, Dushu. They had managed to escape and lived only for revenge. Eventually they linked up with other survivors, and finally they had found (or been found by) Krakanna's forces, which they had immediately joined. It was amazing to speak to four-teen-year-old jasons who had known nothing but the life of a soldier for five or six or even seven years.

During my second day there, Krakanna took me to the Ramsey National Park. As we drove in through the main gate, I saw the remains of the devastation that Labu's goons had caused, and further on there were piles of bleached bones where they had used herds of Thunderbulls for target practice. There were a few avians in the sky, and a couple of small animals in the trees, but by and large my overwhelming impression was one of desolation.

We drove about five miles, then turned off the track and headed toward a dense patch of bush. Finally he parked the vehicle just short of the bush and waited.

We sat motionless for almost half an hour; I was wondering what it was we were anticipating, and then suddenly he grabbed my shoulder and pointed at a movement behind the nearest patch of foliage—and suddenly, nine stately, majestic Thunderbulls paraded past, on their way to water.

Like everyone else, Krakanna had thought all the Thunderbulls were dead, and was thrilled to find out that he was wrong. These nine had been so widely dispersed that they might never have found each other in a park as huge as this one, but Krakanna's people managed to drive them together, and now there is a breeding herd of two males and seven females. He told me he longed for the day when there would once again be thousands of Thunderbulls in the park, possibly all descended from these nine, and observed by tourists from a hundred different races.

Personally, I don't think he gives a damn about Thunderbulls as such; he sees them as a way to rebuild the tourist industry and attract hard currency and put jasons to work—but on the other hand, I don't think his motives are as important as the end result, which will be to both save the wildlife and re-establish a necessary industry.

I know I have had my enthusiasms in the past, but I truly believe that in Krakanna I have found the one jason who might yet save this planet. I have agreed to help him, to act as his go-between with the Republic, and suddenly I'm excited, because for the first time in too many years I'll *be doing something to help, rather than just wringing my hands.*

It will be dangerous, but I feel alive again!
Love,
Arthur

Twenty-nine

As if Faligor didn't have enough problems, it found itself visited with another during Sibo Dushu's reign. Villagers and city-dwellers alike began dying by the dozens, then the hundreds, and ultimately the thousands, with the villagers hit the worst. The symptoms were always the same: the victim would begin slurring his speech and limping, and within weeks or months would gradually lose control of his body until he could no longer walk or even feed himself. The muscles began to atrophy, and no amount of exercise or medication could strengthen them. Eventually, since he could not even masticate, he starved to death. Even those victims who were moved to hospitals and given intravenous fluids were unable to handle them, and the end was always the same: a grotesque, skeletal corpse.

At first it was known as the Thinning Sickness, and finally, when doctors diagnosed the nature of the disease, it received its official name, an acronym that actually described the effects: SLIM, for Subclinical Lusinemia-Imperiled Metabolism. But while doctors understood the effects of the disease, they still had not discovered the cause.

One Christian sect declared that this was God's punishment, that the jasons were a sinful and wicked race, but it didn't make many converts, since most jasons, whether they felt sinful or not, were convinced they had already undergone their share of suffering and then some.

Barioke, for his part, had ignored SLIM, but by the time Dushu took over the reins of power it was too widespread to ignore. Since he was not only the president but the leader of the military, and a beleaguered military at that, his only thought was to find a way to harness the disease and spread it among Krakanna's followers, but since medical science hadn't yet determined the cause of it, nothing ever came of his efforts.

Soon various relief organizations learned of SLIM's existence, and sought permission to land on Faligor and treat the victims. Dushu tried to turn their offer to his advantage, and explained that he could not guarantee their safety under the present conditions, but that if James Krakanna and his followers would throw down their arms and surrender, he would welcome all the humanitarian aid he could get.

Krakanna's answer, not surprisingly, was to blow up two munitions dumps and a subspace transmitting station, and that was the end, at least temporarily, of the relief organizations' efforts to help Faligor's SLIM victims.

It was when two of Dushu's sons came down with the disease that he sent a private message to Krakanna, offering to call a temporary truce long enough to let relief and medical workers land on Faligor and start treating SLIM victims. Krakanna answered that if Dushu's army would throw down their arms and Dushu himself would surrender control of Romulus and Remus, Krakanna would be happy to allow the workers to land, but there could be no truce. After all the abuses and bloodshed, he would accept nothing short of total surrender.

And that is where things stood five weeks after Arthur Cartright returned from James Krakanna's headquarters.

Thirty

The actual battle was brief but bloody.

Krakanna attacked before dawn, striking not at Remus, which was closest to his position, but at Romulus, which was not as heavily fortified. By the end of the day the fall of Romulus was inevitable, but it took a week of house-to-house fighting before the city was secured and his army moved on to Remus.

Cartright had delivered his message to the Republic, which sent a large contingent of medics to the system but kept them in orbit even after Romulus had fallen. They were not about to risk a single human life on this crazed, bloodthirsty planet, and they refused to land until Cartright could guarantee them that Dushu's government had fallen and that the streets of both Romulus and Remus were safe.

The attack on Remus was even more savage. The children fought without fear and without mercy, their war cries sounding like the ululations of females above the din of battle. Four hours into the fighting, Dushu realized that his forces were going to lose, and he quietly left the city along a pre-arranged escape route, accompanied by his most trusted advisors and a handful of bodyguards.

As with Romulus, even after the city had fallen, Krakanna's troops were faced with house-to-house battles for the next three days. When it was obvious that victory had been achieved, the Republic finally sent down its medical teams, which found that they had their hands full right on the battlefield before they could even begin to go into the hinterlands among the SLIM victims.

Thirty-one

D
ear Miss Beddoes:
     I regret to inform you of the death of Arthur Cartright. He was instrumental in our efforts to free Faligor from the yoke of tyranny, and he devoted himself to our cause right up until the end.

     He was shot and killed by a sniper as he was escorting a Republic medical team through the streets of Remus on a humanitarian mission to aid the wounded of both sides.

     As you know, he had no family, and he had willed all his belongings to you. We are holding his effects until such time as you can retrieve them, or direct us in their disposition.

                Regretfully,
                J. Krakanna, Acting President

V

CARBON

Interlude

You work on the Jason children, stabilizing four, losing one, not a particularly bad percentage given their initial appearance, and then you walk away, overwhelmed by the death and destruction all around you. You are a doctor, you have spent your life with the sick and the injured, but you have never encountered them in these quantities before.

Determined to get away from the carnage for just a few minutes, you wander off to the south end of town, but as you approach the savannah just beyond the edge of the city you see huge earth-moving equipment unearthing a grave that must hold five hundred decayed corpses. You wonder which of the three crazed presidents was responsible for this, and then shrug: does it really matter?

You realize that there is no escape from the dying and the dead, and you head back toward the city center to see if you can be of further use. As you do so, you come to a medical clinic. It is a small building, and you enter it, *wondering if there are any wounded who might have taken refuge here.*

The building is empty. The scattered instruments in the operating room are primitive by your standards, the supply of drugs and medications almost nonexistent. The recovery room isn't much better; the "bed" is actually a converted kitchen table.

The roof has caved in, and there is dust everywhere. When you concentrate you can still hear the crack of distant rifles, the hum of laser weapons, the gentle purr of sonic pistols being trained in different directions.

Once again you mutter the question aloud: "How did it come to this?"

And you are startled to receive an answer in thickly-accented Terran.

"Come in here," says a voice from the recovery room, as you jump, startled by its presence, "and I will tell you everything you want to know . . ."

Thirty-two

"Come in here, and I will tell you everything you want to know."

I walked into the recovery room, and found an old jason sitting on the bed, his back propped up against the wall.

"Have you been wounded?" I asked.

"No," he replied. "I came in here when I saw the medics leave after the roof was hit. It seemed safe." He paused and twisted his lips into a smile. "Why would anyone bomb a hospital twice?"

"I'm still trying to figure out why they'd bomb it once," I said.

"Because it's here, and Sibo Dushu isn't going to leave anything for the next president to use." He slowly swung his feet to the floor. "I'm sorry that this had to be your first view of Faligor. It was once a very beautiful world."

"I should be getting back to my work," I said. "There are still victims to be tended to."

"You look exhausted," said the jason. "Sit down and rest. There will still be victims when you leave here."

It occurred to me that I *was* exhausted, and I sat down on a chair and took my helmet off.

"My name is Winston Maliachi," he said. "I am pleased to make your acquaintance."

"I am Captain Milton Papagolos," I replied.

"Captain? I thought you were a doctor."

"A military doctor."

"How long will you be stationed here?" asked Maliachi.

"As long as it's necessary," I said.

"Let us hope it is a long time."

"I beg your pardon?"

"Neither side will risk shooting any Men. They don't want the Republic interfering."

"As a matter of fact, we came here at the request of James Krakanna," I pointed out.

"Really?" he said. "Then perhaps he won't be as bad as the others."

"You were going to tell me about all this," I said, indicating the destruction in the street. "How does an intelligent race choose three successive genocidal maniacs for leaders?"

"You are laboring under two misapprehensions," said Maliachi. "First, we didn't *choose* them, and second, they weren't maniacs. Not all three of them, anyway."

"The one who received all the publicity back in the Republic was Gama Labu," I said.

Maliachi nodded. "Well, he *was* crazy. Not at first, but eventually."

"And the other two weren't?"

"No."

"How can a sane being kill off millions of his countrymen?"

"Expediency," answered Maliachi.

"Expediency?" I repeated.

"Oh, yes, Captain Papagolos."

"Tell me how the hell all this can be justified by expediency."

"I can't," he said. "I can only tell you how *they* justified it. It is an interesting story." He paused. "And when I am done, I will have a favor to ask of you in return."

"What favor?"

"It can wait."

"Ask it now," I said.

He shrugged, sending almost hypnotic ripples across his golden fur. "All right," he said. "The events I am going to recount to you have left me without a family, a job, any money, or even a roof over my head." He paused. "During the length of time that you are stationed on Faligor, you will need help: a servant, a cook, an interpreter, perhaps a guide. I will be all these things for you, in exchange for food and shelter, and, if you can afford it, a nominal wage."

"I don't need a servant," I said. "Or any of those other things, either."

"I wasn't asking on *your* behalf," he said wryly.

"You won't find it demeaning?"

"Certainly I will," he replied.

"Then why—"

"It's been a long time since I was demeaned on a full stomach," he said. "I can learn to adjust."

I shrugged. "All right, Maliachi," I said. "You've got a deal."

He thanked me and the proceeded to give me a brief but thorough synopsis of Faligor's recent history, from the beginning of Arthur Cartright's well-meaning experiment through the progressive terror of Labu, Barioke and Dushu. He told me of James Krakanna's long years in the wilderness, living off the land and the charity of impoverished villagers, waiting for his army to grow both in numbers and age, and how he had finally mobilized against Sibo Dushu.

"We have learned not to put too much trust in our leaders," concluded Maliachi dryly, "nor to hope too optimistically for a better future, but hope is nourishment for the soul, and our souls have had very little sustenance for the past decade, and so, despite all of our recent history, we hope once again. Perhaps Krakanna will keep his promises, or at least some of them."

"Have you any reason to believe he will?" I asked.

"He seemed an industrious and honorable being when I knew him, but that was many years ago."

"You knew Krakanna?"

"I went to school with him."

"What did you do for a living?"

"I taught philosophy at Sabare University," he answered.

"And now you are reduced to being the servant of an alien being," I said sympathetically.

"No, Captain Papagolos," he replied. "I have been elevated to the rank of servant."

"Elevated?"

"It is more than I was an hour ago."

"What did you say you taught?"

He smiled. "My specialty was pragmatism."

Thirty-three

It was his pragmatism that had kept Maliachi alive. It taught him never to trust a politician, so while all his colleagues were listening to Labu's promises, he was already preparing for the worst. He learned protective coloration, and while all the other intellectuals were being murdered, he was able to pass himself off as a peasant farmer. Since he couldn't farm, he became an adept thief, and since the people he lived with had nothing to steal, he eventually went back to the city to prey upon politicians.

In a totalitarian society, the most valuable commodity is information, since the government guards it so jealously. For the past four years Maliachi had kept alive by obtaining information and selling it. Nothing big like military secrets, since there was no market for them, but little things, things people like myself who had grown up in a free society never thought about, like which stores were selling tainted food, which tax collectors could be bribed, and which tribes were about to fall into disfavor with the government.

So it was not surprising that when I mentioned that I needed a place to stay, Maliachi told me that he knew of a house that had recently become available, if it hadn't been destroyed in the fighting. It turned out to have belonged not to a jason but a Man, Arthur Cartright, about whom Maliachi had told me so much.

I protested that we couldn't simply move in, that the estate must still own the house. But Maliachi assured me that it would stand empty until Cartright's heir, who lived many lightyears away, decided what to do with it, and that he would take care of the legalities once the new government's bureaucracy was established. I still didn't like it, but after I found out that the three main hotels in Remus had been destroyed in the fighting, it was either move into the house or stay in our temporary barracks. Being a captain and a doctor were supposed to afford me some advantages, so I finally agreed.

The house seemed in fine repair from the outside, as if the revolution had somehow missed it, but when I opened the door I saw that most of the furniture had been looted. Maliachi assured me that replacing it presented no problem. About the only thing remaining were the book and tape shelves, filled with tomes on sociology, cartography, politics, and a surprising large section on utopian philosophy.

Most of the kitchen appliances were gone, but the

stove and sink, which had been built into the structure of the house, remained, and I made sure that
both the power and water were operative.

"Once, when the house was first built," said
Maliachi, pointing out one of the windows, "you
could see thousands of animals grazing out there. On
a clear day, when the mists rise, you can see the Hills
of Heaven."

"What's a fair rent for the place?" I asked. "I'll
start an escrow fund, and make monthly deposits,
which we can turn over to the owner."

"The banks have all been looted and destroyed,"
he answered. "There is no place to deposit your
funds."

"Then I'll take it out of one pocket and put it in
another," I said firmly, "but I'm damned well going
to pay for the use of the house. Now, what's a reasonable rent?"

"That's a difficult question," he said. "Probably it
would be in the vicinity of a billion credits a month."

"A *billion* credits?" I said disbelievingly.

"Faligorian credits," he explained. "The last time
I saw a loaf of bread for sale, the price was about
fifteen million credits. We haven't had any gasoline
for our vehicles in months now, but it was selling for
about ten million credits a liter when it was available."

"It sounds like your economy was as sick as my
patients," I commented.

"Sicker," he replied. "We went from a barter
economy to hyperinflation in a single generation."

"What will this Krakanna do about it?" I asked.

"I don't know."

"What will he do about the tribalism you told me about?"

Maliachi shrugged.

"What about SLIM?"

"I have no idea."

"If you don't know what he's going to do about all your major problems, why do so many of you support him?"

"We knew exactly what Gama Labu and William Barioke would do," answered Maliachi. "Do you think that was better?"

"No," I admitted. "But surely he's formulated some plans while he was out in the wilderness, waiting for the day he could take over."

"I'm sure he has," said Maliachi. "But he's got a government to form before he starts instituting them."

"Well, he'd better get busy," I said. "If Faligor were a patient, I'd say its condition was critical."

"I'm sure he agrees with you," said Maliachi.

"Then we'll just have to wait to find out if he's the cure," I said, "or simply another symptom."

Thirty-four

J ames Krakanna's image flickered twice on the holoscreen, then solidified and remained.

He was wearing a conservative outfit, the first time anyone could remember seeing him without his battle fatigues, and he was barefoot. He stood behind a small podium, facing a trio of cameras. Just behind the camera were some two dozen jason and alien reporters, all summoned from their other duties to hear the new president's first public address.

"Good evening," he said with no trace of nervousness. "I am James Krakanna, the current Acting President of Faligor. Many of you, far more than the opposition ever suspected, have given me aid and comfort over the years. Many of you have opposed me. Since I am not the egomaniac that my predecessors were, I will even grant that many of you know nothing at all about me."

He paused and cleared his throat.

"To those who have helped my cause, I offer my most sincere thanks. To those who have opposed me, I hereby offer complete and total amnesty for all actions taken up to this minute—but from this minute on, you are Faligorian citizens, and will be expected to obey Faligor's laws. Those laws can be found in the original constitution that was suspended by William Barioke, and is once again in full legal force.

"To those of you who know nothing of me or my beliefs, I am giving this initial speech so that you may know who I am and what I plan to do."

He looked at some handwritten notes he had scribbled down, then stared directly into the largest camera's lens.

"To begin with, all of former President Dushu's soldiers who will surrender their arms must do so by midnight tonight, and you will be set free. After midnight, you will be considered criminals, and will be treated as such.

"Second, anyone found looting anything other than food in any of the war zones will be shot on sight. Anyone found looting food will be arrested.

"Third, all parts of Faligor's original constitution will go into immediate effect, with this one exception: there will be no elections for governmental office until such time as I decide that Faligor's enemies pose no serious threat to her continued existence. At this particular time in our history, continuity is more important than democracy."

"He doesn't sound any different from the rest of

them," I remarked as Maliachi and I watched the speech on Cartright's holo set.

"He's absolutely right," said Maliachi. "There are more important things right now than free elections."

"To those moles who have remained here, or who wish to return," continued Krakanna, "if you can prove that you have spent a minimum of six months living on Faligor, now or in the past, and you desire citizenship, it is freely given, and you will be entitled to all the rights and privileges given to all other citizens of Faligor.

"To those Men who have remained here, we make the same offer.

"To those worlds that wish to re-establish diplomatic and economic relations with us, we welcome you with open arms."

He paused, as if weighing his next statement, and then continued:

"However," he said, "there are going to be some changes. For an entire generation, my people have been known as jasons. We do not consider it a pejorative, and we understand that it comes from Man's mythology—but we are not Men, and the term is no longer acceptable. From this day forth, we are Faligori. I understand that it will take some time for people who have lived here to adjust, but starting thirty days from today, the use of the term 'jason' will be considered a misdemeanor and punishable as such.

"You will also notice that I am not wearing shoes. The reason is simple: our feet are not shaped like

Men's feet, and shoes are uncomfortable and restrict movement. We will assimilate what is useful from other cultures, but we will no longer pretend to be something we are not. The Faligori have no need to be ashamed of ourselves, or to blindly imitate a race that, while it has been a staunch friend from time to time, is no better than we are."

Krakanna paused as applause drowned out his next line, and I turned to Maliachi. "He sounds aggressive," I noted.

"He wishes only to restore our self-esteem," answered the jason. "Do you consider that aggressive?"

"I think he might have stated it more diplomatically," I said.

"He has assumed command of a planet that is used to following orders," said Maliachi. "In a year, if all goes well, they will question those orders, but today they will not, and he must start somewhere."

I grunted a noncommittal answer, as I didn't want to argue, and turned my attention back to the screen.

Krakanna had agreed to accept questions from the journalists who formed the bulk of his live audience, and one of them asked when he was going to disarm his children.

"Never," he said firmly. "They are better disciplined than any military force that has ever existed on Faligor, and they grow older every day. We need them to keep the peace."

"But—"

"Next question?"

"What do you plan to do about SLIM?" asked an alien journalist.

"As you know, Faligor's treasury is bankrupt," answered Krakanna. "As soon as we can replenish it, we'll begin a research project to determine the cause and cure for SLIM. In the meantime, while we cannot pay for their help, we will gladly accept any input the Republic or any of the independent worlds wishes to give us. Next question?"

"You've captured three of Dushu's top generals. What do you plan to do with them?"

"I haven't decided yet."

"Will you release them?"

"I told you: I don't know."

An old Enkoti stood up. "The Enkoti have suffered more under the previous regimes than any of the other tribes. Will your government make restitution to us?"

"My government is only a few days old, and is not responsible for your situation. We can't afford to compensate every victim of Labu, Barioke and Dushu." He paused. "I am sorry, but I won't make promises that I can't keep."

He answered a few more questions, then announced that he was off on a tour of Romulus to make sure it was secure, and that was the end of the news conference. I deactivated the holo and turned to Maliachi.

"He sounds as opinionated and power-hungry as all the others," I commented.

"He is merely a good Faligori, not a perfect one," said my companion. "And it is true," he added, removing his torn shoes, ''that these things hurt our feet.''

''So you're not a jason anymore and you no longer have to wear shoes,'' I said. ''What else has changed?''

''Give him a few months to put his plans into practice before you start criticizing him, Captain Papagolos,'' replied Maliachi.

''And then?''

''Then we shall see.''

Thirty-five

It took almost a month to finish treating all the war victims in Remus, the area to which my company was assigned. At that point most of our medical forces were transferred to other worlds, but the Republic requested that a small number of us remain to work on SLIM, and since I was comfortably ensconced in Cartright's house (and Maliachi, true to his word, had arranged for me to stay there legally), I agreed to stay behind on Faligor.

Once the equipment we requested began arriving, we knew it was only a matter of time before we pinpointed the cause of the disease. After all, we already knew the symptoms, and we had more than enough tissue and blood samples to work with.

But the more we studied it, the farther we seemed to be from a solution. We tested every staple foodstuff of the Faligori; everything was negative. We tested imported human foods. Negative. We tested the mutated crops that the first settlers had brought with them. Negative.

We tested every variety of livestock. Negative.

Water, soil, clothing. Negative.

We then hypothesized that the virus had spontaneously generated within a single Faligori and was transmitted sexually. Negative.

By touch. Negative.

Airborne. Negative.

We went back and began retesting, first the most likely sources, then the less likely sources, and finally the least likely sources.

That was when I found it, embedded in the DNA of a plant that occurred all over the planet. But I had never seen anyone eating it, or using it for medicine, or indeed making any use of it whatsoever.

So I brought a few of its leaves back to Cartright's house with me, showed them to Maliachi, and asked him if he knew whether the Faligori ever used them.

He stared at them for a long moment, then turned to me.

"This can't be the cause of SLIM."

"Why not?" I asked.

"We've been using it for thousands of years," he said. "And SLIM is a very recent thing."

"The plant itself doesn't cause the disease," I explained. "But it carries a virus that does. Probably the virus mutated and became deadly ten or twelve years ago."

He frowned and stared at the leaves again. "I do not know whether God hates the Faligori, or whether He simply has a malicious sense of humor."

"You know what they're used for?" I persisted.

"I do."

"Good," I said. "Whatever it is, we can put an end to it and start making some inroads against the disease."

"It is not that simple, Captain Papagolos," he said. "Things are never that simple on Faligor."

"What are you getting at, Maliachi?" I asked.

He picked up a leaf. "We smoke this," he answered.

"I've never seen a Faligori smoking anything," I said. "Not a cigar, not a pipe, not a cigarette. Nothing."

"It is part of our coming-of-age ritual, one of the most holy and sacred rites in our culture," he said. "A number of the leaves are ground, almost to powder, and wrapped in yet another leaf. During the ritual each boy plus his sponsor, who is usually but not always his father—especially since so many fathers have been killed—smokes the leaf."

"Why?"

"It is both a narcotic and a mild hallucinogen," answered Maliachi. "The rest of the ritual is very painful, and so personal that I do not feel comfortable describing it to you. But smoking the leaf makes it tolerable."

"If it's a narcotic, why haven't your people become addicted to it?"

"The aftereffects are not very pleasant," said Maliachi. "One's stomach cramps up, and one vomits ceaselessly for three or four days. It is not an experience you would want to repeat for a few moments of pleasure.''

"And this ceremony only involves boys?''

He didn't answer, and I asked again.

"It is a very private ceremony,'' he replied. "I should not be discussing it with an outsider.''

"Damn it, Maliachi, your people are dying by the thousands!'' I said. "I have to know!''

He considered it, then sighed and nodded his head. "It involves the boy, his sponsor, his family, and the village priest.''

"But only the boy and his sponsor smoke the leaf?''

"That is correct.''

"Is the sponsor always a male?''

"Always.''

I frowned. "Then how the hell do females come down with SLIM? They've got a twelve percent incidence. Just picking it off the bushes shouldn't cause that.''

"They are the ones who grind the leaf to powder,'' suggested Maliachi.

"You're suggesting they inadvertently inhale some of the powder?'' I asked.

"I'm not even saying that it's inadvertent,'' he replied.

"It fits the demographics of the disease,'' I admitted. "It occurs far more frequently in the countryside than the cities where most of the Faligori have turned their backs on their tribal customs. And if one female prepares a number of the leaves, and not all females inhale the powder, that also explains why so few females are stricken." I considered the theory, and nodded my head. "I think that's the answer."

"It is the answer, but it is not the cure," said Maliachi.

"What are you talking about?" I said. "All we have to do is make sure I'm right and then make the information public."

"And then what?"

"That's it," I said. "We tell the Faligori how the disease is contracted, and explain to them that they must stop smoking the leaf."

"Just like that?" asked Maliachi.

"I don't understand what you're getting at," I said. "We know the leaf causes the disease. You've told me how it's used. All they have to do is stop."

"And if they don't?"

"Why wouldn't they?" I said. "SLIM has killed more than a million Faligori. Nobody who displays the symptoms lives more than five years; most die within six months."

"They have smoked the leaf for untold millennia," explained Maliachi. "It is part of their culture."

"If they keep smoking it, it'll put an end to them *and* their culture," I said. "If they won't stop voluntarily, even knowing that it's the cause of SLIM, then Krakanna will have to outlaw it."

"If he does, I may kill him myself," said Maliachi.

Sometimes, when you live side by side with an alien, when you share your house and your meals with him, you begin thinking of him as just another human being in an odd-looking body. Then something happens, something like Maliachi's last statement, and you suddenly realize just how very alien his race is.

"Why in the world would you say a thing like that?" I demanded.

"Because he has promised that we will be Faligori, and not imitation Men."

"You will be *dead* Faligori," I pointed out.

"Even so."

"You don't understand."

"No, Captain Papagolos," he replied. "It is you who do not understand."

"Then enlighten me."

"Once, within the memory of some still alive, this was a rich and beautiful and abundant world. One by one each of Faligor's treasures was taken from us, sometimes with the best of intentions, sometimes with the worst. But throughout it all, the one thing no one could take was our pride in our identity. If Gama Labu and William Barioke and Sibo Dushu could not make us ashamed to be Faligori, neither can SLIM."

"It's not a matter of shame, but of survival," I said.

"We have survived worse."

"There *is* nothing worse."

"Certainly there is," said Maliachi. "We could become Men."

Thirty-six

When the medical team was absolutely certain
that we had pinpointed the source of SLIM,
we went to work on a vaccine and an antidote—and
ran into a stone wall. The only thing we found that
killed the virus was so potent that there was no question that it would also kill the patient.

We consulted, via subspace tightbeam, with the
finest specialists in the Republic, but while a number
of them volunteered to work on a solution, they all
agreed that there was no quick or easy way to limit
the disease except for the obvious one: change the
coming-of-age ritual.

When we were finally ready to make our findings
public, I requested an audience with President Krakanna, who instantly granted it, and within three
hours I was ushered into his office and was sitting
across his desk from him.

I explained the situation to him and he listened

patiently, his golden face betraying no emotions. When I was through with my presentation, he interlaced the fingers of his hands and stared at them for a long moment, then finally looked over at me.

"I thank you for the work you have done, Doctor Papagolos," he said. "Faligor is indebted to you." He paused. "I hope you will remain here and keep working on a cure."

"That will depend on my commanding officer, sir," I said. "Scientists all across the galaxy are working to find a cure. But I must point out again that there *is* a way of avoiding the disease right now."

"It's not that simple, Doctor Papagolos," he said.

"Sir, I don't wish to contradict you, but it is precisely that simple."

"You are very young and very idealistic," he said with a wistful smile. "You remind me of another of your race when I first encountered him: Arthur Cartright. He also had only our best interests at heart—but it was his idealism and his meddling that led to Labu and the rest."

"I'm not *meddling,* sir," I said heatedly. "I am telling you how to avoid millions of deaths."

"I know, Doctor Papagolos," he said. "And I appreciate it. Now it is essential that we develop a cure."

"In time I'm sure we will, sir," I said. "But in the meantime, it's essential that we mount a re-education campaign and put it into practice as soon as possible. We'll have to get word to every remote village and—"

"Just a moment, Doctor," he interrupted me. "I thanked you for your work—but this is a Faligori ritual and a Faligori problem. The government will decide what actions, if any, must be taken."

"But if you know how to save them . . ."

"I have not told you how to be a doctor," he said, and there was a hint of steel in his voice. "Do not tell me how to be a president."

I considered telling him that if he didn't make the announcement regarding our findings, I would . . . but some instinct told me that I had pushed him as far as I could, that if I protested or threatened any further that I could very well be looking at the inside of one of Remus' notorious prisons before the day was over. So, puzzled and frustrated, I stood up, thanked him for his time, and left his office.

That night Krakanna addressed the entire planet via the holo and radio. He told them exactly what I had told him. The leaf was the cause of the disease, there was at present no vaccine or antidote, nor were any likely to be developed in the near future. The only way to be certain of avoiding the disease was for males not to smoke during the ritual, and for females not to inhale the leaf powder. But he stopped short of prohibiting the ceremony; he merely relayed what I had told him, and stopped.

"He's utterly irresponsible!" I muttered as Maliachi deactivated the holo.

"Why?" asked the Faligori. "Because he trusts his people to make their own decisions?"

"But if they decide wrong, they'll die!"

"And if they die, it will be because of their own actions. It will be a pleasant change."

"You're as crazy as *he* is," I complained.

"You cannot take away a people's entire culture without replacing it with something of equal value, Captain Papagolos," said Maliachi. "All President Krakanna has done is put the choice back into the hands of those who are most affected by their actions: the Faligori themselves. I assume that many of the urban Faligori will change the ritual or eliminate it from their lives; I suspect that most rural Faligori won't, but at least they will have chosen their fate. It will not have been chosen for them. Is that so wrong?"

"You're dealing with children who don't have the experience to make that decision," I said.

"They are Faligori, and you are not. What gives *you* the right to make it for them?"

I got up and walked out of the house for a breath of fresh air before he could say any more, because I knew what was coming next, and I was getting sick and tired of being compared to Arthur Cartright.

Thirty-seven

M y admiration for Krakanna didn't increase during the next two weeks, as one news item
after another came to my attention.

Item: His children's army, which had been dispersed to keep order across the planet, including the
game parks, had shot and killed a Faligori woman
for poaching a Redbison in the Ramsey National
Park. The woman was the mother of five children,
her husband had been killed during one of Barioke's
purges, and she needed the meat to feed them.

(When I complained to Maliachi that Krakanna
seemed to value the life of a dumb animal above that
of a sentient being, he replied that at this moment in
Faligor's history, the dumb animal was indeed more
valuable, for if the parks weren't protected long
enough for the animals to recover their numbers,
there would be no tourist industry, and tourism had
always been Faligor's second most lucrative source

of hard currency, after its mining exports. And
Faligor needed hard currency.)

Item: Gama Labu, whom everyone thought had
been consigned to the history books, decided in his
madness that he was the only Faligori capable of
saving the planet, put his ship in orbit around
Faligor, and radioed his intention of landing and
taking back the presidency that he had "temporarily
relinquished." Krakanna could have blown him out
of the sky, but instead merely refused him permission to land, and after a week of threats, during
which he ran through most of his food supply, Labu
flew off to Domar or wherever he had come from.

(I couldn't imagine why Krakanna hadn't killed
the architect of so many of Faligor's troubles. Maliachi asked me what purpose it would serve. When I
said revenge and justice, he replied that the Faligori
didn't believe in the former, and that for Labu to live
while others ruled his empire was justice enough.)

Item: Sibo Dushu, once more ensconced in the
Great Northern Desert, attacked a pair of local villages, robbing them of their food and killing all the
inhabitants. Instead of mobilizing the army and wiping out these last remnants of the Labu/Dushu military machine, Krakanna merely posted guards at the
other northern villages.

("You should appreciate the motive behind it,"
Maliachi told me. "Until Krakanna can improve
conditions on Faligor, the people need an enemy to
vent their hatred and frustration upon. If he killed
Dushu, they might turn their eyes to Men next.")

Item: With the help of the Botany Department on

the university planet of Aristotle, I devised an herbicide that would affect only the deadly leaf that caused SLIM. When I offered to make it available to Krakanna, as a means of solving the problem once and for all, without forcing the people to choose between their own culture and any other, he refused it.

It was at that moment I finally knew that, for the good of the Faligori, Krakanna had to go.

Thirty-eight

A week later President Krakanna decided to award medals to "heroes of the revolution", and when the list of recipients was announced, I was surprised to see that Arthur Cartright's name was among them.

The next morning I received word from the government that a Susan Beddoes was flying to Faligor to accept the medal. And since she was the owner of my house, would I please make some arrangement to stay elsewhere during the day or two that she would be on the planet.

I sent Maliachi into Remus to deliver my written agreement, and also to find out when her flight would be landing, so that I could be out of the house before she arrived. For once Maliachi made a mistake (or perhaps, in retrospect, he didn't), and as a result, I drove home from the lab after yet another fruitless day of looking for a cure for SLIM, opened the door, and found myself confronting a woman who appeared to be in her early sixties.

"Who are you?" she demanded as I walked into the living room.

"My name is Milton Papagolos, and this is my house," I said irritably. "Who are *you,* and what are you doing here?"

She grimaced. "There seems to have been a foul-up somewhere. The government told me I would be able to stay here while—"

"You're Susan Beddoes?" I interrupted.

"Yes."

"There *has* been a foul-up," I said. "I wasn't expecting you until the day after tomorrow. I'll pack an overnight bag and be out of here in ten minutes. Please accept my apologies."

"The hotel is full. Have you some other place to stay?"

"No, but I'm sure I can find one."

"That's ridiculous," she said. "There are three bedrooms in this house. You will sleep in your own room, and I'll take one of the guest rooms."

"Are you sure you don't mind? I can always drive over to the barracks."

She smiled. "At my age, the only thing gossip can do to my reputation is enhance it."

"How did you get in?" I asked. "I've repro-grammed the security system."

"Your jason servant let me in," she replied. "Maliachi, I think his name is."

"We call them Faligori these days, not jasons."

"That's a step in the right direction," she said

approvingly. "He said that he had business in town, and that he'd be back later."

"His business probably consists of hiding from me," I said with a chuckle. "He's the one who fouled up the dates."

"Well, Mr. Papagolos," she said, "I was just fixing myself some dinner when you came in. Why not join me in the kitchen, and I'll make another portion?"

"Sounds good to me," I said, following her to the kitchen and sitting down on a wooden chair. "When is the medal ceremony? Sometime tomorrow?"

"So they tell me. But I picked up Arthur's medal today. This was a victory of the jasons—excuse me: the Faligori. They don't need any Men sharing the spotlight." She paused. "I'm still trying to decide whether to take the medal home with me, or place it on poor Arthur's grave."

"What did he do?" I asked.

"Arthur? Oh, a little of everything. Cartography, social planning . . ."

"I meant, what did he do to win the medal?"

"Nothing very much, to be quite honest," she replied. "I believe he manned a subspace transmitter and kept your commanding officer informed about Krakanna's position. At least, that's what he told me he would be doing. Personally, I think they gave him the medal to show that we're forgiven."

"Forgiven?" I repeated. "For what?"

"For what we did to a perfectly beautiful, tranquil world," she answered.

"What *you* did to it?" I said, puzzled. "You brought it literacy and medicine and civilization."

"And if it's lucky, it may survive," she said. "How do you like your steak?"

"I don't know. Medium, I suppose."

She smiled.

"What's so funny?" I asked.

"Oh, nothing," she replied. "For just a moment there, you made me think of dear Arthur."

"How?"

"He was always willing to make huge galactic commitments," she answered me, "but he could never make the little personal ones. Like having his steak rare or well done."

"Tell me about him," I said.

"There's very little to tell," said Susan Beddoes. "He was a sweet, decent man who wouldn't hurt a fly. Faligor was his idea." She shook her head. "Pity."

"What went wrong?"

"Oh, it's a long, long story, and I've probably forgotten a lot of the details. Besides, I was early in and early out. I missed Barioke and Dushu, thank God."

"You're a lucky woman," I said. "You'll miss Krakanna, too."

"He asked me to stay."

"He knows you?" I asked.

"Indirectly. His uncle was the first friend I made here. A warrior named Tubito." She paused. "I suppose I must have met Krakanna a couple of times, but for the life of me I can't remember him."

She set my plate down in front of me, then carried another plate to the other end of the table, set it down, and returned a moment later with a bottle of wine and two glasses. Finally she sat down.

"I haven't thought about Tubito in, oh, it must be thirty years," she said. "He would be proud of his nephew."

"Not if he knew all the facts," I said. "James Krakanna isn't much better than his predecessors."

"Really?" she said without looking up. "How many thousands has he slaughtered?"

"None directly," I said.

"Directly?"

I explained his position on SLIM, and his refusal to accept the herbicide.

"He really refused your help?" she asked.

"Yes."

"Well, good for him!"

"I don't think you understand what I've been saying, Miss Beddoes," I said.

"I understand exactly what you've been saying."

"Then—"

"You've been saying," she continued over my objection, "that Faligor is all through accepting our help, which is what got it into this mess in the first place."

"We had nothing to do with SLIM," I said.

"No, but having delivered them into the hands of three successive genocidal maniacs, you would now rob them of the last vestige of their cultural traditions."

"But he's condemning a million or more of his people to death!" I protested.

"Oh?" she said, arching an eyebrow. "Has he ordered them to kill themselves?"

"No, but—"

"So he left the choice up to them?" she continued. "And you just know that they're going to make the wrong decision."

"Look," I said. "If I see a way to save even one Faligori, don't I have an obligation to do so?"

"That's what our traditions would have you believe," she agreed.

"Well, then?"

"I wonder what the Faligori Bible says?"

"I beg your pardon?"

"Milton, everything bad that has happened to this planet—and that encompasses more tragedy than you'll find in the work of twenty Shakespeares—happened because we wanted nothing more than to help them."

"Maliachi says that, but that's to be expected—he's one of them. I don't see how *you* can say that." I paused. "Did Man create Gama Labu?"

"No," she said. "We didn't create him." She paused. "But we created the conditions that allowed him to come to power." She stared at me across the table. "You're a doctor, Milton. You of all people should know that no matter what hideous symptoms a patient may exhibit, you're looking for a germ or a virus that either created the condition or so weakened the patient that the condition was able to exist.

Well, we're Faligor's germ, and the best way not to bring any further harm to it is to leave it alone."

"But we can do such good here," I said. "We can eradicate so much suffering."

"I know we can," she said. "But we exact too high a price for it. Krakanna seems to know that, even if you don't."

"Krakanna," I said, grimacing. "Sometimes I wonder if he cares as much for his people as I do."

"Why? Because he refuses to let them use you as a crutch? Because he knows from past experience the cost of letting us help, of not allowing his people to solve their own problems?"

"Look, I don't want to spend the night arguing with you, Miss Beddoes," I said. "Let us just agree to disagree."

"Perhaps that would be best."

We finished the meal in silence. Then, later, after I'd spent a couple of hours reading through some medical texts, I saw a motion outside the back door and immediately went to investigate. It was Susan Beddoes, sitting on a porch swing, looking off to the west.

"This was such a beautiful world once," she said. "I wish you could have seen it as it was when I first saw it, Milton. It was truly a diamond in the rough." She paused. "Each time I come back, it is less and less recognizable."

"Did Arthur Cartright invite you here?" I asked.

She smiled. "I was the first. I opened this world."

"You did?" I asked, surprised.

She nodded. "That was my sin."

"If you truly feel it was a sin, why do you keep coming back?"

She looked sadly off across the plains. "That is my punishment."

A few moments later she went off to bed. The next day she hunted up Cartright's grave and placed some flowers on it, and the morning after that I drove her to the spaceport.

To tell the truth, I was relieved to see her go. For reasons I couldn't explain, she made me feel very uneasy when I was in her presence.

After her ship took off, I drove to the lab, pushed all thoughts of her from my mind, and spent the rest of the day working fruitlessly on a cure for SLIM.

Epilogue

James Krakanna sat at his desk, a pile of documents to his left, an equally high pile to his right. He sighed and looked out over the city center.

There was so much work to be done, so much more than he had anticipated out there in the forest, when his enemies were Barioke and then Dushu—tangible, palpable living beings. Now his only enemy was failure, for while Faligor could live with Dushu's army in the north and the disease that was eating away at its core, it had hope for the future again, and the only thing it couldn't tolerate was another undermining of that hope.

How did I chance to be sitting here? he asked himself. *I'm just a schoolteacher. I never aspired to the presidency, never wanted it, and now I seem unable to relinquish it. I suppose it is that while my skills may not be up to the task, my vision is clear. I see where we came from and where we are, and I see where we must go. It is a twisting, winding road with many obstacles, but we must traverse it, and we must do so on our own.*

We have come a long way since Susan Beddoes first met with the Sitate Disanko. It is but one lifetime, yet it has encompassed almost five million lives. We have had a mirror held up to our collective soul, and we have not liked what we have seen there.

I don't know what the future holds for me, or even if I can stay the course—but I know the diamond still exists, washed clean with the blood of my people. It has survived the worst intentions of ourselves and the best intentions of others, so doubtless it will survive me too.

Krakanna sighed again, and he picked a document off the top of the pile. The future would have to take care of itself. His job was here in the present, and it was time to go back to work.

Still, he wished he could be here to see what his world became in the next fifty or eighty years. He was almost certain that he would be proud of it.